NURSE
IN LONDON

NURSE
IN LONDON

JANE CONVERSE

THORNDIKE
CHIVERS

This Large Print edition is published by Thorndike Press®, Waterville, Maine USA and by BBC Audiobooks, Ltd, Bath, England.

Published in 2003 in the U.S. by arrangement with Maureen Moran Agency.

Published in 2003 in the U.K. by arrangement with the author.

U.S. Softcover 0-7862-6048-3 (Paperback)
U.K. Hardcover 0-7540-7767-5 (Chivers Large Print)
U.K. Softcover 0-7540-7768-3 (Camden Large Print)

The text of this Large Print edition is unabridged.
Other aspects of the book may vary from the original edition.

Set in 16 pt. Plantin by Al Chase.

Printed in the United States on permanent paper.

British Library Cataloguing-in-Publication Data available

Library of Congress Cataloging-in-Publication Data

Converse, Jane.
    Nurse in London / Jane Converse.
      p. cm.
    ISBN 0-7862-6048-3 (lg. print : sc : alk. paper)
    1. Nurses — Fiction.   2. London (England) — Fiction.
  3. Large type books.   I. Title.
  PS3553.O544N8875 2003
  813′.54—dc22   2003061341

NURSE
IN LONDON

ONE

"I don't know how much longer I can put up with it, Doctor."

Head Nurse Laura Trotter, usually a model of professional calm, looked as though she expected the world to spin off of its axis at any moment. Shaking her head, nerves and muscles quivering, she voiced her complaint in a tone that combined indignation with accusation as she glanced from Dr. Von Engel to Nurse Holly Brooks and then back to the elderly orthopedic specialist again. "You're simply going to have to do something about that bedlam in 206. Never, in all my years of hospital service . . ."

"You've never seen anything like it. Miss Brooks and I were about to discuss the problem and arrive at a solution." The old doctor finished the sentence for Mrs. Trotter, indicating that he knew exactly what she was thinking and what she would say next.

It was a form of dismissal which the head nurse accepted reluctantly, lingering for a moment in the doorway to the consultation room, her expression saying that she considered the situation hopeless and that she didn't think a mere discussion would result in the radical change she felt was in order. Then, with barely a perceptible shrug of her shoulders, Mrs. Trotter said, fervently, "Well, I hope so, Dr. Von Engel. I certainly hope so."

The doctor waited until the door had closed before he sighed, turning an amused stare at Holly. "What I should have told her is that in all *my* years in Orthopedics, *I've* never seen anything like it, either. Nor, I expect, have you."

Holly settled back in the straight-backed Danish chair, giving her full attention to the gnome-like little man seated across the table from her. Thin, usually unsmiling, Dr. Von Engel's appearance was as quaintly foreign as the slight Continental accent that testified to his Viennese birth and, later, his medical training. A halo of fluffy silver hair surrounded his shining bald dome. His pale-blue eyes protruded out of their sockets to compete with a jutting beaked nose, but not with his receding chin. By aesthetic standards, the elderly doctor would have been considered ugly. To a young nurse who had worked with him, learned from him, and, after two years in the celebrated orthopedic wing of Los Angeles's Owens Memorial Hospital, enjoyed the honor of being a virtual teammate of this world-renowned specialist, Conrad Von Engel was someone Holly looked upon with pleasure.

It had been Dr. Von Engel who had encouraged her to take night-school courses in physical therapy, who had schooled her in understanding the accompanying emotional trauma that was as serious to an amputee, for example, as the physical disability itself. Under his tutelage, Holly had gained an all-embracing knowledge of his specialty, and with it had come not only the respect of the staff, but a self-respect, a confidence, that had not only strengthened her dedication but had enriched her life.

Through it all, in spite of his reputation as a martinet and a perfectionist, and in spite of the rigors of his practice, Dr. Von Engel had been unfailingly pleasant. Holly had only seen him lose his temper once, and that had been when a well-meaning patient, complimenting Holly on "a svelte figure," naturally blond hair that needed only brushing and a few combs to produce an elegant coiffure, "gorgeous brown eyes" and "almost perfect features," had wondered why she had chosen her grueling profession when she could easily have made a career of photographic modeling!

Dr. Von Engel's normally placid face had turned red with annoyance. "A model!" he had scoffed. "A pretty face for people to stare at. Buh! What is *here*," and he had tapped first his head and then the chest region over his heart, "and what is *here*, that you would see wasted? A woman born to orthopedic nursing . . . you would have her sitting before a camera making ridiculous poses?"

It had been difficult to suppress laughter as the little man had illustrated his contempt for "ridiculous poses," striking one artificial stance and then another, twisting his thin and wrinkled face into a series of patently false smiles and pseudo-sultry grimaces. "Buh!" he repeated. And, as if that guttural comment had not fully expressed his disgust, he had added something that sounded like "Vrumph!" before marching out of the room.

He was his calm, controlled self now, even mildly amused by Mrs. Trotter's agitation. "So, we will first discuss the situation that is unique in our experience, and then I will tell you of the more serious concern. My reason for wishing to talk with you, yes? Begin. I have no complaint from nurses on the other shifts. What, then, is so intolerable between the hours of three and eleven?"

"I'm sure Mrs. Trotter told you what —"

"From *you,* I wish to hear it," Dr. Von Engel said pointedly. "Mrs. Trotter is concerned with order in her wards. You are concerned with the whole patient." It was a favorite phrase of his; the doctor had drummed into Holly's consciousness his philosophy of treating the patient's psyche as well as the body, giving as much thought to morale as to medicine. Popping blue eyes stared at Holly intently. "The complaint seemed to revolve around visitors, yes?"

"Streams of them," Holly admitted.

"But our young man is only a visitor in this country! He was here in California . . . how many? . . . two weeks? . . . when the accident occurred. He has already so many friends in Los Angeles? Or they fly from England for the sole purpose to irritate our good Mrs. Trotter?"

Holly laughed, shaking her head. "Lee didn't come from England alone, remember, Doctor? He was here for a series of performances. So, we have the four

11

other members of his group. And we have a girl singer. A general manager, an equipment manager — that's the fellow who's in charge of seeing that all the instruments arrive and the amplifiers are plugged in, or whatever. Then . . . let's see; publicity people, wardrobe people, recording engineers, lighting engineers —"

"Enough!" Dr. Von Engel held up a restraining hand. "Fifty managers it takes to produce . . . *quang, quang, quang.*" He gave his nasal and ridiculing viewpoint of modern rock music. "Did Mozart need a retinue of experts? No. But . . ." The doctor made a gesture of helplessness with his small hands. "But, it is not Mozart who flew around the curves of Topanga Canyon and found himself at the foot of a cliff with his legs crushed under a motorcycle."

Holly closed her eyes for a moment, visualizing the scene. The senselessly wild ride, the crash, the amputation of Lee Watson's right leg and the probably irreparable muscular trauma suffered by the other. Any young man would have found the adjustment difficult; for a singing star in his mid-twenties, a performer whose personal magnetism, physical energy, and exuberance were important parts of his public image, the crippling accident could be catastrophic.

"If you're asking for my opinion," Holly said, "I mean, about all the visitors and . . . some of the crazy things that go on in 206, I'm all for them." She recalled the first week after Lee's operation, when visitors were forbidden and the full impact of what had happened to him came thundering into the young Britisher's awareness. She had been alone with him through the long evenings, then, able to ease his physical pain with prescribed analgesics, but left with only Dr. Von Engel's "whole patient" theories to guide her in easing that other, more agonizing pain. "It isn't just that he's distracted during visiting hours. Sure, it's wonderful that he doesn't have time to think about himself with all that activity around him. But . . . I don't know . . . his kind of friends are good for Lee's morale in a more personal way."

Dr. Von Engel's sparse eyebrows lifted. "More personal?"

"Well, they aren't feeling sorry for him. Not that they're callused, or that they don't wish he hadn't had the accident. But, you know the way most people avoid the subject when they visit a new amputee? Or the way they have to *pretend* they aren't pitying the patient?"

The doctor nodded. "I, myself, am not always a convincing actor. Especially when my patient has most of his life before him and we are both aware of the many ways in which that life will be changed."

"That's just it," Holly pointed out. "Lee's friends are all wrapped up in music. They're like satellites that revolve around him, because most of them make their living basking in his shadow. He's extremely popular in England, you know. A household name, actually. And his group . . . I guess you know they call themselves the Tree of Life . . ."

The doctor scowled uncomprehendingly, and Holly grinned. "That's not as bizarre as some of our homegrown groups. I don't suppose you've heard names like the Peanut Butter Conspiracy. Or Blood, Sweat, and Tears. Or maybe Joy of Cooking?"

"These are *orchestras?*" The Viennese in Dr. Von Engel was offended.

"Sort of." Holly decided to skip the orientation course in modern music and returned to the primary subject. "Anyway, these people were drawn to Lee because they respect his talent. As a vocalist, as a musician, as a songwriter, arranger. Regardless of what you may think of the

14

music, Doctor, Lee Watson is an enormously gifted person. He hasn't lost his talent, and his friends don't let him forget it. Not by *telling* him. They simply come into the room and carry on as though nothing had happened. They play records, they project light shows on the walls; I think they'd bring their instruments and hold rehearsals if Mrs. Trotter would let them."

"And they are not disturbing other patients?" Dr. Von Engel asked. "I am always finished with my evening rounds before the visiting hour begins, as you know. So, I have *seen* some of our young man's friends. Ach, and what a colorful assortment they are! Though if I were to comment on their exotic long hair styles, you would undoubtedly attribute my criticism to jealousy." Dr. Von Engel ran a hand over his bald pate and feigned a tragic expression. "No, no, I wish only to be considerate of other patients. I do not underestimate the value of madness, if madness is my patient's normal way of life."

"Mrs. Trotter's going to hate me," Holly predicted. "But the truth is, the Tree of Life has been a big boost to everybody's morale. Maybe the over-thirty staffers never heard of Lee Watson, but the young patients on our floor rate his group up along with the Beatles and the Rolling Stones. He came to the States for a tour, and it was heavily publicized. Besides, every kid who listens to a rock station or owns a record player knows about Lee Watson."

Dr. Von Engel apologized for his ignorance. Quite seriously, because curing "the whole patient" meant knowing every aspect of that patient's life, he promised to acquaint himself with the Tree of Life albums Holly listed for him.

"And don't be prejudiced, just because you prefer Mozart," Holly warned. "Listen to the lyrics Lee writes. He's a poet, among other things. A poet who communicates with my generation."

That was another thing Holly admired about Conrad Von Engel: he was able to open his mind to new areas, especially if they concerned someone he was trying to help. "I will try to remember that Strauss waltzes were once considered shockingly vulgar," he said.

They chatted for a few minutes about Lee Watson's fellow musicians — the drummer, Harvey Scott, an apple-cheeked, mustachioed younger version of Harpo Marx, except that the curly mop of bright

16

yellow hair was his own; Norb Sutliffe, who played chess when he wasn't thumping the bass, and who wore his mahogany-colored hair in a long, yarn-tied ponytail; the group's organist and vibes player, a metaphysics buff named Desmond White, though he was a native of Trinidad and quite black; and second guitarist Mark Ainsley, the group's youngest, albeit hairiest member, who sported, along with shoulder-length red tresses, a bushy beard that belied his age and made his juvenile addiction to mechanical toys seem doubly ludicrous. They talked, briefly, about Maxine, who was referred to as the group's "singing bird," but whose voice was not heard on any of the three albums they had released.

"She doesn't sing much," Holly reported, "and she doesn't talk at all, except to Lee."

"What, then, *does* this young lady do?" the doctor wanted to know.

"Mostly sits around looking like Sacajawea, and suspicious. I mean, she dresses like her idea of an American Indian squaw, complete with black braids. And, oh, yes . . . she pastes Lee's publicity stories into a scrapbook. I don't think she likes me, but, then, I don't think she likes anybody. Especially if Lee *does*."

"I know he is very fond of you," the doctor said.

It was time to change the subject again. In the past few weeks, that fondness had reached an uncomfortable plateau, and Holly found herself wishing that her patient would be well enough to return to London before Lee Watson's dependence upon her (a dependence and gratitude he was beginning to mistake for love) created a serious emotional problem. "You wanted to talk to me about something else, Doctor," she said.

He tapped an index finger on the medical charts spread before him on the table. "I am satisfied with the healing of the stump. If the other limb were sound, we would be ready soon for our prosthesis fittings. Since the artificial leg will serve, in a sense, a purely cosmetic function, our patient will probably wait until he has returned to his home country before he is fitted."

"You don't think there's any hope that —"

Dr. Von Engel cut the question off with a deep sigh. "I keep looking at the X-rays, consulting with other specialists, hoping. No. No, I am afraid our patient will not regain mobility with crutches. I have told him this, as gently as possible. You and these devoted friends you mention must convince him that his career need not be shattered because he will be confined to a wheelchair. But my grave concern . . ." The doctor faced Holly with a probing stare. "When he is not surrounded by . . . activity, what do you see? How is the morale then?"

"It varies. Anywhere from manic enthusiasm to suicidal depression. None of the moods last long, fortunately." Holly recalled instances when Lee had clung to her hand, wordless, huge tears streaming down his face. "Then, as though someone had flicked a switch, he'll be telling me about his ideas for the next album cover. He's a very complex personality, Doctor. Nothing I've learned about the average patient applies to Lee Watson."

"I agree. And there have been no complaints about phantom pain?" The doctor was referring to the phenomenon in which an amputee feels pain in the toes or fingers of a limb that has been severed.

"No. The pain has been confined to the site of surgery."

Dr. Von Engel frowned. "Which, at this time, should not be sufficiently serious to justify the use of morphine."

"But he insists that nothing but a hypo relieves the pain," Holly said. "Of course, he doesn't *know* he's been getting morphine. He just complains that the pain pills don't help him and he begs for 'a shot,' as he calls it."

"I am not so certain," the doctor said slowly. "No, not certain, at all, that our young man is unfamiliar with analgesic drugs." The doctor's troubled expression was replaced by a determined look. "We cannot risk addiction. If necessary, we will combine an injected placebo, for psychological effect, with a non-narcotic pain reliever. I will leave instructions at the desk." Dr. Von Engel gathered up the papers from the table, talking to himself more than to Holly as he added, "Must add this to the case history I will forward to Dr. Raymond in London."

"Dr. Raymond?"

"Yes, Glenn Raymond. I was able to recommend an excellent orthopedics man to our patient. I have met the doctor at European conferences on two occasions. Read several of his papers in medical journals. With only a few weeks to go before our young man is released, I am pleased that he will immediately be in the care of a specialist who will follow my regimen. It is my hope that he will find a nurse-therapist, also, to continue the exercises."

"But Lee hasn't said anything about going back home soon." Holly rose to her feet as Dr. Von Engel pushed his chair back. "Of course, there isn't going to be a tour, and he's in good enough condition to be flown back. It seems strange, though. Lee confides even minor plans to me. Wouldn't you think he'd have mentioned that he was leaving for London within a few weeks?"

The doctor reached the door, pausing to turn a significant glance in Holly's direction. He was thinking aloud, and he sounded worried as he said, "He may insist upon leaving sooner. When we discontinue the morphine, he may want to leave immediately. I think it's worth a call to London. Warn Dr. Raymond that our patient may have to be closely watched."

Two

Neither Holly nor Mrs. Trotter, the head nurse, had any problem in clearing Lee Watson's room of the usual overload of visitors that evening. One minute, 206 resembled a bon voyage party crowded into a cabin of a cruise ship. The next, after a terse command from Lee ("All right, mates. Everybody split!"), the room was cleared of everyone but the patient, his private duty nurse, and Lee's closest friend and personal manager, Bartie Mitchell.

"Business meeting, luv," Lee explained to Holly. Propped against several pillows in the hospital bed, a light blanket drawn up to his waist, the teenager's idol looked anything but a tragic figure. The long-sleeved madras-print pajama shirt had been tailored expressly for him. His own barber, who traveled as part of the star's retinue, had come in that afternoon to do whatever it was that he did to keep the medium-length wavy brown hair in its faultlessly groomed Edwardian style. ("Conservative Early Beatles" was the way Lee described it.)

Incredibly deep blue eyes, fringed with dark lashes, recalled Lee's Irish ancestry on his mother's side. His longish face, still showing traces of the California tan he had cultivated during the early weeks of his visit, seemed to live a superanimated life of its own, reflecting Lee's changes of mood with lightning swiftness.

But it was not Lee's striking appearance that arrested attention. His charisma resided in a personality that was filled with paradoxes: intense, yet confidently serene; charmingly warm, yet separated from others with the regal aloofness of royalty. You sensed that behind those placid blue eyes, a charge of creative energy was constantly at work. "Dynamic" was a word Holly would have chosen for Lee Watson, though, at various times, almost every adjective in her vocabulary could have been applied to him.

Now he had switched, suddenly, from being the irrepressible life of the party to acting the level-headed businessman, using one of his lanky arms to wave aside Holly's offer to leave the room. "No need," Lee said. "I don't have any secrets from *you*, of all people." He tossed his head back, releasing a short laugh, though, like all of his laughter, it had bitter overtones. Then, in a careless manner, he added, "Bartie and I want a few words to decide what's up with the bird."

"The bird?" Holly responded to a finger signal from Bart Mitchell and placed a can of cashew nuts next to the chair in which he was sprawled, acknowledging his "Ever so kind of you, luv" with a nod.

"Maxine," Lee elaborated, "Bartie had an antiquated idea at the time we were putting the Tree together that you can't set three or four musicians on a platform without having a chickie up front. It was the formula, back in his day, y'know. Bartie didn't have to buy new bell-bottoms and belt-in-the-back suit jackets when they came back into style. He's so old, he simply took his 1930 wardrobe out of mothballs."

"Never saw the thirties." Bart popped a handful of cashews into his mouth. "I was a war baby."

"Crimean war," Lee assured Holly. "Get his autograph, Nurse. He knew Florence Nightingale personally."

Bart addressed his argument to Holly, too. "I'm exactly two years older than my esteemed client. We grew up in the same elegant quarter. Lovely place, wasn't it, Lee?"

"Smashing view of two box factories, a freight yard, and a fishmonger's," Lee remembered. "Actually, we shared the same pram. Can you imagine London surviving the blitz *and* Bartie's arrival in the same year? You see now why they call us the indomitable British? Never mind his age. Mr. Mitchell merely *thinks* like an old codger. Set in his ways, y'know. Big bands playing swing music, with a tone-deaf bird upstage. Rhinestone evening gown and all that."

Bart chuckled. "Listen to 'im. And *'e* was the one wot 'ired 'er nibs!"

Most of the time, Bart spoke in the precise, clipped manner that came so easily to Lee Watson, although both admitted that their cultured Oxford sound was a "recently acquired affectation." But when Bart relaxed, exchanging the friendly insults that usually preceded a serious discussion with Lee, he slipped into the Cockney dialect that was natural to him, perhaps even exaggerating the misplacement and omission of h's.

Somehow, the dialect complemented Bart's appearance. Small and wiry, he moved with the jaunty and uneven motions of a sparrow, although when he was persuaded to sit down and relax, he collapsed like a puppet whose strings have been cut, slouching deep inside his chair. Like his body, Bart Mitchell's face was small and birdlike. He had keen gray eyes that peered at you through rimless specs, thin auburn hair that drooped past his earlobes and managed to look disheveled in spite of the grim attention lavished upon it by Lee's highly paid hair stylist, and, although Bart spoke of having to "look a bit conservative, since I 'andle the business end," his taste in clothes, while expensive, succeeded in making him look more like a racetrack tout or carnival barker out of the thirties than the mod entrepreneur he actually was.

Perhaps the antique eyeglasses, or the plaid knit cap he affected (and which seemed to cut even further his sparse height), gave Bart his older appearance. Still safely under thirty, he was regarded as "the old man of the troupe." Or perhaps his fatherly image rose from Bart's unfailing good sense. A born promoter, doggedly loyal to Lee and the Tree of Life, he had never erred in making moves calculated to advance the group's popularity and income. He was Lee Watson's alter ego, but he was as responsible for the star's success as Lee's own innate ability; Lee might argue with him, poke fun at Bart's expense, or use him as a scapegoat for his frustrations, but he listened to his odd little friend with respect.

"All right, I hired the bird," Lee said. There had been a pause in the conversation and Holly had gotten so lost in introspection that Lee's voice startled her. "That means I can decide that she's expendable."

"Do *you* tell her she's expendable, or do I?" Bart wanted to know.

Lee's face clouded. "I wasn't talking about booting her out, y'know. I simply mean that I can't justify her presence musically."

"Rather a heavy expense to carry if she's going to be confined to cutting your pictures out of fan magazines. We pay a clipping bureau to do that. I should think, if you aren't going to let her sing —"

"You can't simply dump a person who's been that devoted to the cause," Lee cut in irritably.

Bart shrugged. "If she isn't going to be any more than a groupie, she'll be the only highly paid professional one I know about." Bart was referring to the idolatrous girls who followed the popular musical groups and for whom Lee had expressed his contempt.

"Let me think about it a bit," Lee said after a thoughtful silence. "It's not a personal thing, Bartie. I've no sentimental attachment. But I do detest emotional repercussions, and I don't think she's going to be overjoyed by the prospect."

"Righto. I don't relish discarding someone like an old shoe because we made a mistake early in our planning." Bart checked his watch. "How much more time am I allowed, Holly? I have nine-ten."

"You've worn out the welcome mat by ten minutes," Holly said.

Bart stuck his tongue out at her. "Keep that up, they'll promote you to Old Trot's position. Head Terror." He got to his feet, grabbing a fresh handful of cashews in the same coordinated motion. "I'll pop along, old boy. I thought now that you're up to working on songs for the next album, you ought to consider the Maxine situation. It's tacky, what? But if it's going to upset you to get rid of dead weight, don't worry about it. We write her off as a tax loss. And Maxine isn't terribly ambitious. She hasn't gone off in a huff yet, and you haven't written a song for her in more than a year."

"Haven't been writing any for myself lately, either." Lee had moved slightly in his bed, turning his face away from Bart's view. "See you about tomorrow," he said. He sounded falsely cheerful and Holly guessed that he was anxious to have his visitor leave.

"I'm looking forward to hearing that new one you were toying with," Bart said. He stood near the door, awkward, sensing that Lee had become suddenly depressed, and reluctant to leave without stirring up a positive burst of enthusiasm. "What did you say it was going to be? Country baroque. Banjo meets harpsichord. I say, that ought to be —"

"Bartie?" Lee pronounced the name wearily. "Later, eh?"

Bart threw a miserable glance in Holly's direction, but his voice didn't betray his concern. "Righto. Righto. There's tomorrow. The other chaps will want to hear —"

"*There isn't going to be any tomorrow! It's over! Can't you stop playing your idiotic games and see that it's all over?*"

Holly caught her breath at the shrill cry, hurrying to Lee's bedside. "Don't, Lee. Please don't do this to yourself . . ."

"Over! Finished! Kaput!" Lee was straining forward, as though he wanted to leap up and run from the room, his face contorted by agony. "Don't you *see?* What was our image? Joy. Vitality. *The Tree of Life!* Well, the tree's had a limb sawed off, Mitchell!"

Lee's voice had risen to a strident, near hysterical pitch, and Holly brought it down with a sharp command. "Don't do this to *him*, Lee! I don't think Bart deserves it!"

Lee shuddered, perhaps at his own words. Then, in a more subdued tone, but still agitated, he said, "I'm not going to be the freak who does his thing from a damned wheelchair. Gawked at like some ruddy freak. You've got the name. Go on with it."

"You know how far we'd go without you," Bart said quietly. "All right, you don't want to do personal appearances. That's cool. Did you suddenly stop being a musician? There's nothing wrong with your voice."

Lee had gotten control of himself, but he sounded grudging as he argued, "Don't want them buying discs because they've read all that sentimental gush in the fan mags. Gad, they'll have me labeled the Wheelchair Warbler. Long stories about how courageous I am, pity-provoking rot about my refusing to give up. I'm not going to trade on my misery, Bartie. Nor are you."

30

Bart's face flushed, but he was equal to the biting insult. "You're trading on my sympathy *now*, chum. And I'm not wasting pity on a chap who can write fab songs and do fab arrangements. Not when he has five other people depending on him and he'd as soon let all of us down as not."

Bart had chosen the right words for a sobering effect. Defensively, but somewhat sheepishly, Lee growled, "Never said I wouldn't provide material."

"We need the whole bloomin' sound!" Bart exclaimed. "You say you don't want to do personal appearances 'cause you don't want people feeling sorry for you. Right-*o!* Trowbridge cabled 'e's got a date set for a free park concert. To promote the current album. Hit's goin' t' cost 'im a bundle, that. And 'e says 'e wants you, if you 'ave t' do your thing from an *'ospital* bed!"

Lee showed a faint interest. "He actually said that?"

"Got the blinkin' cable right 'ere in me pocket." Bart reached into his inner jacket pocket.

"Never mind," Lee mumbled. "I'll take your word."

"More like it, I'd say! Now, d'ye ever know Keith Trowbridge t' do something

31

out of the goodness of 'is 'eart? To make a few bob for 'is record comp'any, more likely."

"But the crowd he pulls . . ."

"You'd draw them no matter wot!" Bart insisted. "Before or arfter you got yourself in this muddle. Come off it, Lee! Trowbridge expects to pull a hundred thousand. Wouldn't you like to blow their minds with your cornpone harpsichord rock thing?"

Bart's question was like a magical prod. "It isn't rock and it's not really country," Lee explained. "The way it's in my head now . . ."

Lee talked for the next ten overtime minutes about the songs "in his head." Like a gushing fountain, he poured out his idea of what the mammoth free concert should include, how the new numbers would be orchestrated, how the program should be staged. Bart had reopened that vast creative dam, and Lee's infirmity was temporarily washed away in the flood of enthusiasm.

Expectedly, when Mrs. Trotter had opened the door to glare at the late-staying visitor, and Bart had bounced out of the room, Holly was present for the inevitable letdown. Lee closed his eyes, his hand

32

groping for another hand to cling to, someone from whom he could draw strength in the sudden quietness surrounding him.

Holly let him press her fingers in a tenacious grip while she searched her mind for a new distraction. "You've been making wonderful progress, Lee. If you'll just take the therapy seriously . . . cooperate on the exercises . . . you should be up to anything. Even a mammoth free concert."

Lee kept his eyes pressed shut, and Holly noticed that his jaw was quivering.

"Your guitar's in the closet, you know. Bart brought it up last Sunday. I'm surprised you haven't asked for it."

"I couldn't manage."

"Sure, you could."

"I'm used to standing up when I play."

"It's a matter of adjustment, Lee. That's why we have you doing the exercises. Building up . . ."

"Holly?"

She knew what was coming. "Yes?"

"I hurt."

"I'll get the new pills Dr. Von Engel prescribed."

Holly tried to extract her hand from Lee's, but he didn't relinquish the firm hold. "Pills are like peppermints when it's this bad," he said.

"You've built up a tolerance," Holly told him. "This is something new. Let go, Tarzan. I'll be right back."

"Holly, I need a shot." The blue eyes were open now, pleading with her. "I've got to get some sleep if I'm going to work tomorrow."

"You'll sleep. I promise." Holly's fingers ached in the viselike grasp. She found it difficult to maintain a cheery bedside manner. "You'll be out like a light in no time."

"I tell you, pills don't do the trick. A hypo. Who says I can't have that?"

"Your doctor."

Lee was outraged. "What sort of doctor would let a man suffer when —"

"The sort who wants you to . . ." Holly caught her breath; she had nearly slipped and used the stock phrase "to get you back on your feet." She recovered quickly, finishing the sentence, ". . . to get well. With no serious side effects. He doesn't want you getting dependent on drugs." It was an effort to meet that knowing, accusing stare; Lee Watson was accustomed to getting what he demanded. "It's standard medical procedure, Lee. Every doctor varies the pain-killers he uses. Let me get the —"

"I don't want any damned fool pills," Lee said.

Matching his stubbornness commanded all of Holly's will power. When your whole heart went out to a patient, being sensible and following doctor's orders was a strain. That first week, when the dressing had to be changed several times during her shift, she had empathized with Lee so strongly that she had almost yearned for the oblivion of the morphine hypo herself. Now, fighting to keep pity out of her voice, she said, "I can't disobey your doctor's instructions, Lee. You know that."

"Ring him up! I'll talk to Von Engel myself!" Lee's bombastic command withered away in the next breath. "There's no point in it." He released an exasperated sigh, deflated. "Stay with me, then, Holly. I'm in for a rough go."

"I'll stay. Of course I'll stay," she assured him.

"I'm getting out of here soon." Lee sounded like a defiant schoolboy now. "Week or so. No more."

"Why shouldn't you? Dr. Von Engel thinks you're strong enough to go home. You'll be under a doctor's care, but you can manage with a home nurse. I hear your specialist's been selected. Dr. Von Engel thinks very highly of him."

"My nurse has been selected, too," Lee

said. "I rather think Dr. Von Engel will approve of her as well."

"Oh?"

A delicate half-smile played around Lee's mouth. His eyes, crinkling at the corners, had that soul-searching expression known, according to Bart, to have driven a young female audience into screaming hysteria. "I've got you, haven't I?"

"But you're going back to England."

"No matter. Can't very well make the journey without a nurse, can I?" Lee pulled Holly closer to his bed. "I want you, luv. Here, on the way, over there."

"I wouldn't be permitted to work in a foreign country," Holly protested. "You have your own nurses . . . excellent ones, I'm sure, who —"

"Trust Bartie to take care of that sort of nonsense." Lee's handsome face, with its talent for flashing changes, suddenly appeared wistful. "Don't you want to take care of me, Holly?"

"Of course I do, but . . ."

"I was rather hoping you'd want to come along because you *care* about me."

Lee's overpowering personality was not lost on Holly; looking into his eyes was like being drawn by a magnet. Of course she cared. She told him so, finding herself

36

trembling, knowing that Lee expected her to lean down and kiss him, and finding the attraction almost irresistible.

Holly managed to free her hand without being abrupt, repeating, "Certainly I care. If I didn't think you'd have the best medical attention . . ."

"I meant . . ." Lee didn't have to verbalize what he meant. He let those expressive eyes of his speak for him. After a long while, he said simply, "I love you, Holly."

There was another long electric pause, during which Holly struggled to sort out her emotions, trying to separate love from pity. There were so many factors at work here, she reminded herself; the natural bond that grows between two people who have gone through trying times together, the compassion of a private nurse for her patient, the ego-satisfying importance of being needed, and, finally, the flattery of being singled out by the exceptionally attractive idol of thousands of girls, girls to whom Lee's handicap would be only a minor consideration. This was *the* Lee Watson saying that he loved her. Even the knowledge that he might be mistaking gratitude for love didn't erase Holly's breathless sensation.

"You don't have to commit yourself,"

Lee said. Before embarrassment could rise in Holly (had she been silent that long?) Lee did another of his lightning changes, turning on a grin that was all boyish charm and saying, "Let's not make it a grim thing, luv. I'm thinking of what a fabulous holiday we could make of it. London's not a stuffy place; old colonels sitting about their club drinking bitters, or old ladies in floppy hats serving tea at garden parties. London's a pacesetter now, y'know. It swings. I want to show it to you. Soon as I can get around . . . and I *will* get around, one way or another, I'll show you London the way no tourist ever gets to see it."

He painted a glowing picture of parties, celebrities who were his close friends, theaters and quaint shops. Lee described his home city with the excitement that he had poured, earlier, into the monologue about his music. When he had described enough attractions to make Holly want to run home and pack her suitcase, Lee asked, "Is there any reason at all why you shouldn't come along? You don't have a family problem."

It wasn't a question; Holly had already told him about her parents, who operated a small café in a desert town a three-hour drive from Los Angeles, and Lee had autographed albums for her two younger sisters. "No, I . . . I've been living away from home since I started my nurse's training. No hang-up there."

"And there's no steady fellow." Lee made a statement of this, too, rather than a question.

Holly smiled. "No one who couldn't manage without me."

"*I* can't manage without you," Lee said. "That's it, then. Far out! You're going to London, Holly girl!"

Lee had a few moments of manic enthusiasm, followed by nearly two hours of pleading for the painkilling morphine injection Dr. Von Engel had forbidden.

Shortly before she went off duty at eleven, Holly talked her patient into taking the pills that had been prescribed as a substitute. Lee fell asleep, clinging to Holly's hand, minutes before the night nurse reported for duty.

"Thank heaven he's not awake," the night nurse whispered. "The few times he's been awake when I came on, it was like a nightmare."

Holly was nearly out of the room when the middle-aged R.N. who relieved her added, "I've never known a patient so dependent on one nurse. Mr. Watson's going to have a difficult time when he doesn't have you supervising his therapy and getting him to cooperate. I must say, he truly needs you, Miss Brooks."

It was a clinching argument, added to Holly's own excitement over the prospect of being part of a new, exciting scene overseas. It only remained for Conrad Von Engel to add his encouragement the next day, dismissing Holly's concern that Lee Watson's dependence upon her was *too* personal.

"You are worried that you will hurt our young patient by rejecting him, is that it?" The doctor shook his white-haloed head. "No, no. As soon as he is in his own milieu, he will no longer lean on you emotionally. A complete rejection now . . . yes, this would be demoralizing. Later, he will see you in proper perspective, eh? It is this period of readjustment that is so crucial, Holly. To prevent him from becoming addicted to a narcotic, to keep his morale high enough so that he does not refuse to follow the routine of exercises; this appears to be within your power. We are dealing with a sensitive but extremely strong personality. Your presence at this time could mean the difference between recovery and total collapse."

An appealing adventure had assumed the proportions of a sacred duty and there was no more convincing needed. Mrs. Trotter, clucking her tongue disapprovingly, was notified that Holly would leave the hospital at the time Lee Watson was released.

It wasn't necessary to tell Lee of her decision; he had assumed that Holly would accompany him to London at the time he made his request.

THREE

Preparation, after Lee had announced (and Dr. Von Engel had approved) departure in only ten days, would have been hectic without Bart Mitchell's advice.

As semi-official trouble-shooter for the Tree of Life, the jaunty little genius, with his curious off-and-on Cockney accent, not only was able to provide Holly with all the information she needed regarding her passport, shots, etcetera, but, since he managed Lee Watson's finances, relieved Holly of her last-minute shopping worries. "You aren't going to Pango Pango, ducks. 'Alf the fun of the capital's shopping, and you won't be lacking for quid."

Earlier he had told Holly he was securing her work permit. Bart had also informed her that her present salary would be doubled, and, as with the rest of "the Tree's staff," all her living expenses would be paid.

Still, it didn't seem that he was talking about Holly's generous salary when he added, "You won't ever have to worry about buying whatever strikes your fancy, old girl. Not ever."

Holly questioned him about that strangely melancholy statement, privately wondering if Lee had spoken to his eccentric little manager about future matrimonial plans. Again, curiously (because Bart Mitchell was not known for being taciturn!), he refused to go into detail, deftly changing the subject when Holly pried for an explanation. He raved about the mod shops along Carnaby Street, was as enthusiastic as Lee in describing the new trends that had made London the new Mecca for tourists, and spared no adjectives in whetting Holly's appetite for the adventure before her.

Most of Lee's entourage, including the other four members of the Tree of Life, welcomed Holly to the fold with varying degrees of interest. The one notable exception was Maxine, who lacked, along with a family name, the ability to generate enthusiasm for anything. She stared at Bart Mitchell blankly when he told her that Holly would be accompanying the group to London.

"It's going to be my first trip outside of California," Holly told her, hoping to stir up some spark of a rapport with the tiny

British version of Pocahontas.

Maxine's dark eyes gazed at her unseeingly through heavily mascaraed lashes. "I don't mind," she said after an interminable pause. Her intonation suggested that she couldn't care less. But, later, when Lee let it be known to his troupe that Holly meant more to him than "just a bird who takes care of me," Holly caught the stabbing glance of jealousy that Maxine darted in her direction.

Nor was there any reason for Maxine to feel resentful because she was being drummed out of the corps. Oddly (or, perhaps, *typically*, since no one could account for Lee's contradictory impulses), not only had Maxine not been dismissed, but Bart had been asked to sign her to a new two-year contract! It was none of Holly's business, and she asked no questions, but it struck her as unusual that a singer who wasn't going to be allowed to sing should be retained at a high salary, especially when Lee and Bart had agreed that she was "quite expendable." That the tiny, dark-haired girl who affected fringed suede miniskirts and beaded headbands was in love with Lee Watson seemed obvious enough to Holly, even though Maxine appeared capable of no more emotion than a zombie. But why Lee should elect to have the songless songbird around was a mystery, unsolved by Bart's blithe explanation: "Lee wouldn't 'ave the 'eart to send 'er packing." This dedicated loyalty to obsolete employees was especially confusing to Holly when she learned that Harvey Scott, Lee's Harpo-haired drummer, had only recently replaced the percussionist who had been a part of the Tree of Life during its lean beginnings. Furthermore, the former drummer had been dismissed on a day's notice, his only sin being that he wasn't as good as Harvey!

Jealous or not, expendable or not, Maxine presented no problem. Holly's first negative reaction to her new job came from other quarters, and it came with the impact of a hurricane when the BOAC jet landed at London's Heathrow Airport.

A heavy fog swirled over the airport as Holly, flanked by an airline stewardess and Bart Mitchell, started to push Lee's wheelchair down the specially ordered ramp. It had been a pleasant flight. Everyone aboard had been in exceptionally good spirits, and Holly's only concern over her patient had been with Lee's exuberance. Excited by the homecoming, it had been impossible to separate him from the irrepressible high jinks of his friends. Instead of resting, Lee had been the life of the jet-borne party. "It's been too much of a strain for Lee," Holly complained. "I hope we can get him to a quiet room in a hurry."

"Don't worry, now," Bart whispered. "It's all set. Ambulance waiting. I've 'ired two 'usky orderlies to 'elp with getting Lee in and out of bed — that sort of thing. They'll 'ave 'im resting in his suite before you can say Ringo Starr."

Holly leaned forward to make certain that Lee was riding comfortably. "Well, you're home, sailor! And no more whooping it up until you've had a good, long rest."

She remembered hearing Lee laughing, then making some quip about the London fog being better for her complexion than that "parching California sunshine." Then the nightmare horde descended upon them.

A shrill chorus of feminine voices rose up to greet them. There were cries of "It's Lee!" "He *is* on this plane!" "Let me through, I want to see him!" The backs of two uniformed bobbies appeared out of the fog, and Holly saw that they were attempting to hold back a pushing, shoving mob of girls.

Lee, who ordinarily took a dim view of screeching fans, let out a gleeful howl: "My public! What a welcome home!"

"Get back into the plane," Holly yelled to the passengers lined up behind her. "Help me pull the chair back!" Except for the stewardess, who made an attempt to follow the order, no one paid any attention to Holly. Lee's entourage waited patiently for his wheelchair to move forward, perhaps still unaware of what was happening. Even Bart stared ahead, looking only mildly surprised at the ruckus, ignoring Holly's plea (if he heard it at all above the tumult a few yards ahead).

"Bart, please! Lee's going to be mobbed if —"

"*I say! Halt! Halt!*"

One of the girls had ducked under a policeman's extended arms and was pitching forward toward her idol. Her success evidently inspired her sister fans; the squeals reached an ear-splitting pitch and there was a wild surge forward. One of the bobbies tumbled backward, grabbing the rail before he fell to the platform. In the next instant the mob would have trampled him if he had not clung to the banister. They rushed forward, a mindless wall of humanity, shrieking Lee Watson's name, too frenzied to be reasoned with.

In the moment between that break-through and the time that the first of Lee's worshipers clambered up the wide ramp, Holly had slipped around to place herself between the wheelchair and the girls. *"Bart . . . stop them! He'll be hurt!"*

This time, Bart responded to Holly's desperate cry. He was at her side then, joined by Desmond and another man she didn't recognize, all of them forming a protective cordon around Lee.

"I just want to touch him!" one of the girls cried. "Lee! Lee!"

Her hysteria was echoed by the others: *"I love you, Lee!" "All I want's a lock of 'is 'air!" "Get out of the way, we didn't come to see you, Nursie!"*

Breathless, her heart pounding, Holly begged, "He's just had surgery . . . don't you see . . . oh, please . . . please don't crowd . . ."

Bart and the others had taken up the chorus. "Don't crowd! Step off, please! Lee will talk to all of you . . . you'll be able to see him if you step back to the field!"

Words were futile. Holly found herself shoving, pushing away the arm of a girl who had crouched down in an attempt to grab at Lee's shirt, using her elbow to block a panting teenager who was endangering everyone by waving a scissors in her insane quest for a lock of Lee's hair.

Several bobbies had joined the fight from the rear, waving nightsticks, pulling back some of the stragglers, ordering everyone to get off the ramp. But the forerunners of the mob were too close to realizing their dream to be deterred. Pretty, ugly, fat, thin, blond, brunette, redhead; they were uniform only in their frenzy. They seemed incapable of reasoning, unable to recognize the fallacy of endangering a man's very life while paying him their fanatical homage.

Holly had a momentary flash of recollection: Lee Watson telling her during one of their long talks at the hospital of the sprinting escapes he had made from stage door to waiting limousine. Saying, "Those vultures would tear you into bits and take the carnage home to glue into their memory books. Some of them terrify me, really. All you can do, unless you're trapped, is to run, head down, like a rugby player."

Lee's reference to "running" had brought an abrupt, painful ending to that conversation. But it came to mind now as Lee sat helpless behind her, totally at the mercy of his "adoring" fans. Apart from the danger of physical injury, there was now the trauma of finding himself face to face with his helplessness. Heaven only knew what this horror would do to his morale.

The thought of it goaded Holly into fury. She smacked with her open palm at a girl who was trying to push an autograph book and a sharp pencil through the human wall surrounding Lee. Another girl made a clawing gesture at her face, an attack that was, fortunately, deflected by the towering organist from Trinidad. Apparently the girl had an ally; Holly cried out in pain at the sharp jab of a pencil against her midsection. Blinded by tears, screaming as loudly as her attackers now, she flailed at them with her fists. A quick glimpse revealed that Bart Mitchell was being overwhelmed by pummeling females. The bobbies, outnumbered by a fresh wave of screaming girls, were faring as badly. In another minute, Lee's defenders would be pushed into his lap. It was like a zoo in which all of the animals had been crowded into a small cage and had gone berserk.

It would have seemed impossible for a single voice to rise over that piercing din.

But Holly heard the sudden shout: a female voice that came from somewhere behind her, yet in the wild confusion could have come from anywhere in the crowd:

"This isn't Lee Watson! It's a double! There he goes! They're sneaking him off that other jet!"

There was an electrifying silence, followed by a disgruntled murmur from the girls on the ramp. Then someone else (and this time Holly recognized Mark Ainsley's voice, in spite of the female impersonation) shouted, "They can't do this to us! Let's go!"

Miraculously, the fans Holly had been fighting off responded like sheep, turning to race after a group that had apparently decided their hero was debarking from another airliner. Shielded from view by Bart and several others, Holly managed to get the wheelchair back into the plane.

Bruised, unnerved, her heart pounding, Holly would have collapsed in tears if she hadn't been conditioned to think first of her patient.

Ironically, Lee seemed to have survived the ordeal better than the others. Bart's nose was bleeding and a furrow of three fingernail marks had been raked across his left cheek. The dark-skinned organist's lower lip was swollen, though he seemed to have suffered more damage to his clothing than to his body; Desmond's flashy orange tunic was in shreds.

Nevertheless, Holly gave her first attention to Lee. "I was afraid they were going to trample us to death."

Like everyone else aboard, Lee was breathing hard, but unlike his companions, he was smiling. "Quite a go, wasn't it? I'm fine, thank you. Better patch up old Bartie, there." Lee's grin broadened as he addressed his manager. "Rather a smashing success, wouldn't you say? I've got to hand it to you, man. You may be a smashed pugilist, but you're a smashing publicist."

Later, while Lee dozed and they waited for the disappointed fans to disperse, Holly cleaned Bart's scratched face with an antiseptic solution. Bart winced as she daubed a soaked gauze pad against the raw scratches. "I was a little disappointed in Lee," she said. "After the battle you and Desmond put up to protect him, I would have expected him to say thank you."

Bart shrugged. "Lee's done enough for us to be able to take things like that for granted. Ooh . . . what are you painting me with, luv? Muriatic acid?"

"I know it hurts, but you can't risk infection. That's a nasty souvenir that little girl left on your cheek." Holly continued the rough cleaning process, still dissatisfied with Bart's reaction. "I know you're friends and you assume that the other fellow will come to your rescue if you need help. My point is, Lee wasn't just unappreciative. He acted as though the whole thing was a lark. As though he *enjoyed* it. And you know, he could have been seriously injured in that crush. Even killed. He actually looked *pleased*."

"Of course he was pleased. You're concerned with healing the body, ducks. I know how important it is to preserve that precious artistic ego." While Holly prepared a gauze bandage and cut strips of adhesive, Bart expanded on that theme. "I'll admit it was a bit hectic there for a bit. Hysteria, and all that. But our boy came out of it *happy*, y'know. Think 'ow crushed 'e would have been if not a bloomin' soul 'ad showed up to greet 'im."

Holly looked at the satisfied expression on Bart's comic face. Incredulous, she asked, "You didn't *plan* to have that pack of females here, did you? Bart, you couldn't have!"

"Survived it, all right, didn't we?"

"Answer the question! Did you let the

press know when and where Lee'd be arriving?"

Bart pursed his lips for an instant. "Let's just say I didn't classify that information as top secret. Lee needs medicine for the soul, too, don't forget."

Holly's experience with the crushing mob was too fresh in her mind to be dismissed that lightly. Anger stirred inside her. "You *assured* me that Lee would be resting in his room a few minutes after we landed. I never dreamed you'd expose him to anything that . . . insane and dangerous. He's still far from recovered. If someone hadn't diverted those maniacs . . ."

"Maxine," Bart said in a bland tone. "Clever girl. Waited until the telly photographers got good shots of the rush, and then did her thing about our hero going thataway. Trust that bird to know what's right for his nibs."

"Well, no more!" Holly flared. Oddly, the compliment to Maxine had added to her anger, as though she were in competition with the silent songbird, as though she had entered a cheap contest to see who could be of the most service to Lee Watson! "If I'm going to be responsible for Lee's condition, he's going to be protected from this sort of thing. Bad enough to go through it when you're strong and well, but weeks after a major amputation? No more, Bart! If you want to take the responsibility, fine — go right ahead — but I'm not going to stand off another screeching pack of vultures. Lee's going to get proper care, or I may as well take the next plane back to the States."

Bart made no promise and gave no encouragement, only staring at Holly in a half-bemused, half-melancholy way, as though she didn't know what she was saying. Holly took a softer tack, appealing to his fondness for Lee. "You don't want anything bad to happen to him, do you? It's just that you don't understand, when a patient's undergone drastic surgery —"

"A few things that *you* don't understand, luv," Bart cut in. "About what's really important to Lee. About what he needs to keep him going."

Holly taped the dressing to Bart's cheek, her fingers far from steady. "Oh, I'm sure you know a lot more about what's necessary for Lee than I do." Her sweet sarcasm thickened as Holly added, "You and Maxine."

In spite of the smarting pain of the scratches Holly had just dressed, Bart stretched his face in a wide grin. It laste

55

only a moment. Then it was replaced by a sober, almost sorrowful, look. "As a matter of fact, luv, we do."

Unaccountably, Holly found herself throwing supplies back into her first-aid kit. Why should she be furious? Because other people were more important to Lee than she was? Not that it was true; hadn't Lee begged her to stay on as his nurse? Hadn't he said that he *loved* her?

"You don't get to know someone as complex as Lee in a few months," Bart went on. "I've known him since we were this high" — he indicated the height of a toddler with his hand — "and I still don't know him, really. Sometimes I'm not even sure I like him. Does that surprise you, Holly? Love the type; might, if you'll excuse the mellerdrama, might lie down an' die for 'im. And don't mind being *used*, the way he uses every one of us. But I *do* know Lee's a user. Fortunately, the Maxines — and they've come and gone, remember — the Maxines and I know he uses us. We're hip to it and we don't mind, because we're rather in awe of what he can do. That fantastic talent. His power and influence over our generation and the generation just coming up. He communicates in a way only a handful of people do in one lifetime." Bart slipped his steel-rimmed specs back on. With the dressing on his face, he looked like a soldier newly returned from a battlefront. "So, you see, we don't really mind. We bask in reflected limelight, you might say. Gain a bit of importance vicariously, and count ourselves lucky to be a part of his scene. But we know where we stand, ducky. And to stay where we are, we've got to know what's necessary for Lee."

Holly scowled, but she was not left untouched by the revealing confession. She tried to maintain a bristling pose. "That elephant stampede out there was 'important' to him, I suppose?"

"Quite," Bart said. "I wouldn't have arranged it if I hadn't thought it was exactly what Lee needed to keep him going."

"Well, he's had his ego bolstered," Holly conceded. "Now will you see to it that it doesn't happen again?"

Bart was still gazing at her as though Holly hadn't begun to understand his point. "It won't happen again," he assured her. They started up the aisle to the forward section of the plane, where Lee Watson rested in his wheelchair. In a quieter tone, Bart qualified his promise: "Until it's necessary again. The way it was necessary today."

Four

There had been a two hour delay before Lee Watson and the Tree of Life could safely be transported from the airport to their hotel. Holly had known a moment's panic, looking out the ambulance window as they neared their destination and seeing another riotous crowd of young people, evidently intent upon gaining entrance into the hotel lobby. But Lee's craving for recognition had been, at least temporarily, satisfied, and Bart had arranged to circumvent the second welcoming reception. From the ambulance, which had been driven to an underground garage, Lee was spirited to his suite by way of the hotel's laundry room, a series of gloomy service areas, and an elevator usually used for furniture.

Holly's sigh of relief, when they closed the door behind them in Lee's sumptuous quarters, was clearly audible. "I don't think I'll try to get rich and famous," she told Lee. "What a price to pay for fame."

Lee was being helped into an Oriental silk lounging costume by a towering young man who had been introduced to Holly as Rajah, and whose darkly regal aspect qualified him for the title. Speaking softly when he spoke at all, he lacked only a turban and an elephant to complete his image.

As the powerful East Indian who was to serve as Lee's daytime orderly lifted the star from his wheelchair and gently settled him on the mammoth bed, Holly opened the case containing supplies she would need for changing her patient's dressings.

"It took a bit of adjusting," she heard Lee saying. "Even when you aren't rushed, there's always someone staring at you. Can't drop into a pub or browse in little shops. I didn't realize how precious privacy is until I lost it."

"I wouldn't like it one bit." Holly carried a tray of the needed gauze and a fresh "stocking cap" stump cover to Lee's bedside. "I'd hate the loss of freedom . . . not being able to walk down the street without —"

"That won't be a problem with me any more," Lee said curtly.

Holly's careless reference to walking brought a rush of blood to her face. "I'm sorry, Lee. You know I didn't mean . . ."

"I'm sorry, too," he said wearily. "It's a natural thing to say. I oughtn't embarrass you this way. You shouldn't have to weigh every word. Next thing you know, I'll stop asking the chaps to 'run' through a number with me." Lee made a hollow laughing sound, trying to make a joke of the sensitive issue. Then, while Rajah moved around the room soundlessly, opening wardrobe trunks without so much as clicking the locks, arranging Lee's voluminous wardrobe in the mammoth closets without the faintest rattle of a hanger, Holly changed the dressing, avoiding Lee's eyes as she did so, painfully conscious of his watching eyes and his agonizing silence. When she had folded back the trouser leg and pinned it in place, she said, "It's healing very well. Can't be giving you too much trouble — you haven't asked for so much as an aspirin since we left the hospital in L.A."

"Been too busy to think about pain," Lee said lightly. "So fab, being at home."

Unconsciously, Holly glanced around the suite, its luxury completely impersonal.

"Oh, this isn't really home. I've a marvelous house out in Kent, but with the concert coming up, Bart thought this would be more convenient for rehearsals and whatnot. Besides, it's being remodeled. My house, I mean. The workmen didn't expect me back quite so soon."

It seemed impossible to get away from references to Lee's accident; if the Tree of Life had completed its American tour and gone on to Australia, as planned, Lee would have been away from home several weeks longer.

He looked wistful for only a moment, however, and then explained, "I meant it's good to be back in London. You haven't given me your impression. Do you like it?"

Holly laughed. "So far, I haven't seen the city for the fans. With the curtains drawn in the ambulance . . . well, actually, I *did* see that huge Los Angeles-style hotel near the airport. But what I've seen of the view from your window is exciting. Is that the Thames?"

"Righto."

"Skyscrapers, too. Hardly my idea of Old London Town."

"You'll see that, too. I've asked Bart to see that you get your fill of musty palaces and that sort of thing. If you get homesick for smog, he'll spin you over to Manchester. Sorry about London Bridge. It's been dismantled and shipped to America . . . some vast new development in the desert. I understand some Texas oil bloke has placed an order for Westminster

61

Abbey. And I think . . . yes, Buckingham Palace has been carted off to Disneyland to make room for a row of U.S.-style hotdog stalls."

Holly smiled. "You're so tired, you're mad."

"Happy's the word." Lee reached out to catch Holly's hand. "I only wish I could show you the city, luv. But, then, you don't like being trampled by the Watson Fan Club."

Holly feigned a shudder. "I never thought of pencils as weapons before."

"They'll be especially hostile when they learn you're my girl. Can't you just hear them? *'There's the bird 'e chose instead o' me!'* " Lee waved an imaginary weapon above his head. " *'Arfter 'er! Wop 'er wit' yer autergraph books!'* "

Even Rajah caught the playful spirit, indulging himself in a polite smile as he carried an empty wardrobe trunk to a storage closet. It was pleasant to have Lee in this joyful mood, although the overstimulation of the trip and his homecoming reception was probably responsible. Dr. Von Engel had warned against letting Lee exhaust himself, and there was no doubt in Holly's mind that her patient was running on pure nerve.

She crossed the room to draw the heavy velvet draperies, the brief glimpse of a spectacular view of London reminding her that she was in a colorful foreign city. Somehow, the hectic arrival had obscured that exciting fact. "Time for a nap, Mr. Watson." She smiled at Lee's orderly. "You're in charge, Rajah. Nobody, but *nobody*, is to get past that door until Lee has had at least two hours of quiet. Check?"

Rajah nodded amicably.

"Now, wait a minute," Lee protested. "There's one person I want to see . . . for just a second or two. Could you hand me the phone, Holly?"

Holly scowled, but she placed the bedside telephone within Lee's reach.

Lee gave her a sheepish glance. "I just wanted to thank somebody for getting us out of that mess at the airport." He seemed to be hesitant about picking up the receiver, looking at Holly as though the call were personal and he wished she would leave.

Holly started for the door. There seemed to be an uneasy, even guilty aura surrounding Lee's call, and the immediate need to thank some individual, especially since he hadn't bothered to thank Bart, Desmond, or Holly for their protective stand, was hardly typical of Lee, who was generous with friends and took their loyalty and services for granted. Still, if he hadn't wanted Holly to know about the call, he could have waited until she had left the room.

As Holly opened the door, she heard Lee saying to the hotel's switchboard operator, "Connect me with Maxine's room, please." Then, after a pause, snapping irritably, "No, she doesn't. She's registered under her Christian name. M-A-X-I-N-E."

It wasn't until Holly had closed the door behind herself in her own room, conveniently located across the hall from Lee's suite, that she wondered why Lee couldn't have extended his thanks to Maxine on the phone. Perhaps he intended to, yet he had distinctly said there was one person he wanted to *see,* and he had addressed the statement to Rajah, who had been charged with seeing that no one was admitted to the room.

It wasn't her business, Holly decided. Lee had a gift for keeping his tribe intact and contented. Maybe he sensed that Maxine was miffed over being relegated to second place in his affections. Or, having discarded her as a singer, he still recognized her devotion to his troupe and felt that she should be pacified. Whether Lee was concerned with the girl's sensitivity, or whether he was thinking bad public relations would result if she left the group in a huff, it was his right to thank her for the quick wit that had diverted that mob at the airport.

Apparently Maxine responded to the summons in record time. Holly heard a knocking on the door opposite her own a few seconds later. Lee held to his promise to keep the visit short; not more than three minutes elapsed before Holly heard Maxine's voice saying, "Righto, luv. You can always count on me, y'know," and then the door being closed.

It was a trivial incident. Why, then, should she be (in Lee's own parlance) "getting bad vibes" from it? I'm tired, Holly decided. She was even too worn out for more than a cursory examination of the lovely room that had been assigned to her, with its mellow oak paneling, lush olive-green carpeting, and marbled adjoining bathroom. Her luggage had been delivered to the room. A warm bath and a change of clothes appealed to her, but getting off her feet presented a greater temptation. Holly sank down on the bed, slipped out of her shoes, and mentally calculated the time she would have for herself before Lee's pre-dinner therapy. Three hours, at least, and she was sure that Rajah could be depended upon to see that Lee got his needed rest.

Luxuriating in the prospect of having no one to worry about except herself, Holly stretched out across the bed, her mind reviewing the thrill of her first transatlantic flight and projecting forward to sightseeing in London, with Bart Mitchell as her tour guide. Lee had said that his manager would show her the city. Yet Bart would be busier than ever now that he was back in England. When would he find the time to . . .

A ringing telephone startled Holly. As it rang the second time, she realized that she had drifted off into sleep. For how long? She reached for the receiver, a quick glance at her wristwatch revealing that she had slept no more than ten minutes. Her groggy "Hello?" was mingled with a sigh of relief.

"Sorry to disturb you, Miss Brooks," a crisp feminine voice said. "There is a Dr. Raymond to see Mr. Watson. Mr. Watson's attendant left word that he's not to be disturbed. The doctor's asked if he might see Mr. Watson's nurse."

Holly considered inviting the doctor up

to her room, then decided against it. "Please tell Dr. Raymond I'll come down in a minute," she said.

A quick splash of water was substituted for the leisurely bath, and Holly's change of clothing was limited to the addition of a fresh scarf to brighten her travel-wilted suit. If Dr. Raymond was anything like Conrad Von Engel, he wouldn't notice if she appeared wearing a burlap feedsack; the important matter was not to keep him waiting.

Holly regretted her decision the moment she entered the sedately furnished hotel lobby. If the strikingly handsome young man who approached her as she stepped out of the lift was Dr. Raymond, an hour's wait while she made herself more presentable would have been justified.

"Excuse me. Are you Miss Holly Brooks?" The deeply resonant voice with its cultured intonation accompanied a hesitant smile.

It *was* the doctor, though from his tall, athletic build, Holly would have pegged him as an outdoorsman. Mahogany-brown wavy hair with neatly groomed sideburns framed classic features and a pair of serious, yet extremely alert dark-brown eyes.

Too overwhelmed for anything more

than a nod, Holly stared at the man stupidly as he said, "I'm Glenn Raymond. I expect Dr. Von Engel told you I'd be looking after young Watson now that he's here in London."

"Yes, he . . . he told me you would be."

"Is something wrong?"

Holly flushed. "No, I . . . no, nothing at all." Impulsively, and regretting her words midway through the sentence, she added, "I was expecting someone like Dr. Von Engel."

Glenn Raymond looked perplexed for a moment, perhaps even a bit resentful. "I assure you that I'm quite qualified," he said stiffly.

"Oh, I don't question your qualifications!" Great! She had gotten off to a fabulous start! "I just meant . . ." What could she say now? Explain that Dr. Von Engel was a funny-looking little old man, and that she was stunned by Dr. Raymond's youthful, movie-star appearance? He would have been more embarrassed, probably, than she was now. Holly settled for saying, "Forgive me. It's been a rather . . . hectic day. I'm not thinking too clearly."

Only faintly miffed, but still looking as reserved as his conservative dark suit, white shirt, and navy-blue tie, the British doctor asked, "Are you up to introducing me to our patient? I could return at a more convenient time."

That slight edge of sarcasm didn't help. "I'll be happy to introduce you to Mr. Watson," Holly said, sounding more like a starchy old head nurse than herself. "I think I can even manage to recall his room number."

There was an awkward silence, and then the ludicrousness of their touchy exchange struck both Holly and Dr. Raymond as funny. He laughed shortly, and Holly covered her face with her hand, laughing too, and feeling like a champion fool. "I usually make more sense," she assured the doctor.

"I'm sure you do. Dr. Von Engel isn't lavish with compliments unless he's sincere."

Another pause, and then Holly said, "We had a stormy reception at the airport, and Lee . . . Mr. Watson was exhausted. He's resting now . . . probably asleep."

"In that case, I won't disturb him. This happens to be the one afternoon and evening I'm free, so it won't be inconvenient to return." His hopeful glance threatened Holly with another awed stammering session. "Are you on duty now?"

"Not really. I try to be available at all times, but there's a qualified orderly in charge now."

"I thought perhaps you could tell me something more about the patient," Dr. Raymond said. "From the case history I've read, Mr. Watson's made excellent physical progress, but there seem to be a few . . . psychological problems."

"Well, he's a . . ." How did you describe Lee Watson? "Lee's an extremely complex and sensitive person. For a while, he was convinced that his career was shattered."

"Doesn't believe that now?"

"At the moment, no. But he's a mercurial personality. I can't be sure what he's thinking from hour to hour. A sort of manic-depressive thing."

"I see." It was getting uncomfortable, standing in the way of hotel guests walking between the registry desk and the elevators. Dr. Raymond nodded toward the restaurant adjoining the lobby. "If you can spare the time, we might have our discussion over a cuppa."

"A . . . ?"

"Tea," he explained. "I could use a spot. Could you?"

Holly smiled. "I'll have to develop the habit. At the hospital in Los Angeles, we

70

did everything but take baths in coffee. Would I be a rude guest if . . ."

"Coffee it is, then, for you." The doctor had closed his hand over Holly's elbow and was guiding her across the busy foyer, probably unconscious of the devastating effect of his touch. "My landlady can't brew anything properly, so I've probably never had a decent cup of coffee. Fortunately, good tea isn't hard to come by, once I've gotten off Mrs. Trelawney's premises."

He couldn't have known the impact of that innocent banter. If the doctor was dependent on a landlady for his tea, it was a safely optimistic guess that he wasn't married. *Why* didn't I change to my lime-green knit? Holly wondered. She cursed herself for not having daubed on lipstick; not even the saving grace of a powderpuff run over her nose!

Ironically, during the idle get-acquainted conversation that preceded their discussion of Lee Watson, Glenn Raymond made a disparaging remark about women who used too much makeup. He was looking directly at Holly, stirring his tea absently, as though he were aware of nothing except the girl seated on the opposite side of their cozy corner table. "You were prepared for an octogenarian," he said. "I was expecting what you Americans call the old razzle-dazzle. It's such a bore to have to probe through layers of goop to discover what a woman looks like. I expected a stereotype image, you being fresh out of the Hollywood area. Isn't it pathetic, the way we tend to classify foreigners before we meet them?"

Holly nodded. There was a surge of relief at not appearing as dowdy as she had thought. In fact, the young doctor's appraisal of her face was so approving that she felt a warm glow that, hopefully, radiated from her. More at ease now, she said, "I grew up believing all Englishmen wore tweeds, puffed on little briar pipes, and said 'harrumph' between every other word. The Tree of Life cured that impression in a hurry."

"We don't all hunt foxes, either," she was told in an amused tone. "Or play chess in stodgy clubs." Dr. Raymond refilled his teacup from a small china pot. "This is the only cliché that will hold up. We *do* slosh around in tea, though, speaking for myself, I've never eaten a cucumber sandwich and I detest crumpets."

Their talk led to a discussion of Lee's group and the bizarre clothing they affected, the mad pace at which they lived. "I know that Lee Watson can't help driving himself," Holly said. "It's almost as though he's been trying to cram a hundred lifetimes into a few short years. He wants to see and do and experience everything, without pausing for a breath."

"His accident was apparently part of the syndrome."

"Yes. It's slowed him down in mobility, but not in any other way. The problem at the hospital was getting Lee to cooperate with Dr. Von Engel's regimen — and ordinary hospital routine, for that matter — without depressing him. We had to be flexible; realize that thumping rock music and his wild friends were as vital to him as . . . say, get-well cards and potted chrysanthemums would be to an elderly lady recovering from surgery."

"I've written a few papers on the subject," Dr. Raymond said.

He looked mildly amused again, and Holly suspected that she had managed to make a fool of herself once more. Dr. Von Engel had *told* her, hadn't he, that his theories about treating "the whole patient" were compatible with those of the English physician? Here she was, explaining the fundamentals of a subject on which Dr.

Raymond was a published authority!

Mercifully, he was not patronizing as he said, "We'll try to be flexible, of course. However, in the serious matter of dependency on specific analgesics . . ."

"Oh, I don't think we have that to worry about any more," Holly cut in.

"Really?"

"I think getting back to normal activity has done the trick. Confined in the hospital, Lee had too much time to think about his physical problem. He's so enthusiastic now about getting back to work that he hasn't given a thought to drugs. Promised to take a nap without asking for so much as a sleeping pill."

"I expect you'll keep careful note of what he *does* ask for," the doctor said. "Now, then, tell me how you've been progressing with therapy. After I've had a look at the patient, we may want to make a few changes in the exercises. You've had him continuing the push-up, lying on the abdomen at least twice a day?"

Holly filled him in on her progress, and occasional lack of progress, explaining the times when Lee Watson refused to cooperate. "If Dr. Von Engel had been able to do a flap-type amputation above the knee, and if there hadn't been hopeless damage to the other leg, the stump would have been completely healed by now and we'd be fitting Lee for a prosthesis. As you know, the trauma was so extreme that it had to be a quick guillotine operation. Between the slower healing and the fact that Lee doesn't really have enough incentive to exercise . . . you understand, I'm sure. The artificial leg isn't going to serve anything more than a cosmetic purpose and Lee knows it. Makes it difficult to urge him to develop muscle tone when there's so little to promise him."

"He knows he can't vegetate," Dr. Raymond said. He spoke in a positive manner that indicated he was a man who accepted compromise if it seemed reasonable to him, but expected his orders followed to the letter when it did not. Unlike Dr. Von Engel, who would sometimes vacillate over thorny problems where either solution had advantages and disadvantages, the younger doctor struck Holly as one whose swift mind made firm choices and tolerated no deviations from the course he charted. "If Mr. Watson's going to go on with his career, he's going to have to concern himself with his general health. That will require not less, but more, exercise. I'll expect you to be patient but quite firm about this."

Holly shook off a fleeting resentment, reminding herself that this authoritative newcomer to the case was charged with the principal responsibility for Lee's welfare. Dr. Raymond eased that brief moment of tension, too, by changing the subject, asking questions about Lee Watson's plans, talking about the "Watsonmania" that seemed to be approaching earlier Beatlemania proportions, and, finally, chuckling over Holly's report of how Dr. Von Engel had, in the interest of his patient, listened to recordings by the Tree of Life. "It must have been a painful experience for the poor chap." Dr. Raymond shook his head from side to side dolefully. "I can hear him asking himself what the world's coming to! I've never discussed music with Von Engel, but I can well imagine his reaction."

They were exchanging stories about the American doctor's eccentricities, chatting as easily as old friends, when Holly realized that over two hours had elapsed since they had come into the hotel restaurant. "We should be able to go up now without disturbing him," she said. "You must be anxious to get back to —"

"I have no commitments for the evening," Dr. Raymond said as he signaled for the check. He hesitated for a second or two before adding, "I hadn't made dinner plans, for that matter. I gather your hours on duty revolve around medication, dressings and therapy?"

"Yes. Now that I have two round-the-clock male nurses to help."

"If you're free this evening, I'd enjoy having dinner with you. Continue our discussion." Before he could let Holly conclude that the invitation was purely social and perhaps even a bit presumptuous, he added, "After I've examined the patient, I expect we'll have more to talk about."

"I'm sure of that," Holly agreed. She left the dining room in an ecstatic state, hardly aware that she had been exhausted several hours ago, and unconcerned that there would be no time for sleep between now and the unexpected dinner date.

Her joy ended in the corridor outside Lee Watson's hotel suite.

FIVE

Even before Holly and Dr. Raymond had turned into the hallway leading to Lee's quarters, the din assailed their ears. Rock music and the hubbub of loud voices filled the corridor.

"I hope . . . that racket isn't coming from Watson's *room?*" the doctor asked.

A waiter, pushing a cart of liquor bottles, glasses, and an ice bucket, was knocking on Lee's door, supplying the answer to Dr. Raymond's question.

Tight-lipped and apprehensive, Holly followed the waiter into a room in which a full-scale party was in progress. Under a haze of blue smoke, the bizarrely dressed band members mingled with a conservatively outfitted group Holly had never seen before. A stereo system, which had not been present when Holly had left the suite, blared the Tree of Life's most recent album, competing with the chatter of voices, bursts of laughter, and the clink of ice cubes in highball glasses. Bright lights, television cameras, and a network of cables added to the confusion.

In the center of activity, his wheelchair resembling a throne around which a private universe revolved, Lee Watson carried on an animated conversation with several men who, Holly guessed, were reporters.

Rajah, helping to clear a path for the waiter, inched his way through the crowd. Catching sight of Holly, he made a helpless shrugging motion, indicating that he'd had no power to prevent what was happening.

Holly shoved past the waiter to where Bart Mitchell, Maxine, and a group of strangers were standing. Bart greeted her enthusiastically, "*There* you are, ducks! I've just called your room, wondering why you weren't here."

Before Holly could protest, she was being introduced to four members of the press and a simpering, overdressed female columnist for an American fan magazine who was asking, "Miss Brooks? Can you tell our readers how Lee reacted when he was told that he would never walk again?"

"How do you *think* he reacted?" Holly snapped.

The woman made a gasping sound, and while she glared her indignation, one of the male reporters asked, "What's it like, having the job every girl dreams about?"

Holly's irritation chose Bart for a target.

"What's going on here, Bart? When I left Lee he was going to rest. This is —"

"It's Lee's press party," Bart said. "Lovely turnout, what?" He turned an amiable smile at the miffed lady columnist. "You might say, Cornelia, that Lee never lost his determination to keep bringing his music to his fans. 'E loves those kids as much as they love him."

Cornelia thought enough of that touching revelation to set her cocktail glass inside a plant pot, the only square inch of space available, freeing her hands to fish a notebook from her handbag.

"Have you ever worked as a private nurse for any other celebrities?" another of the fan-magazine snoops wanted to know.

"I'm not going to be working for *this* one, unless I can get some cooperation," Holly said. "Bart, he isn't well enough to stand a pace like this!"

Bart made a kind of pleading signal with his eyes, and then proceeded to pacify the reporters with the sentimental-heroic-titillating information they were seeking. Holly's mouth fell open as she heard herself described as a former Hollywood starlet who had given up a glamorous career in order to serve humanity. Someone had turned up the volume on the stereo set, and it was getting impossible to hear voices or to be heard, but as Holly spun away from the group, she heard Bart saying, ". . . saved the Maharani's life during a yacht explosion in the Bahamas, but Holly's terribly shy about personal publicity . . . won't even discuss a possible romance with Lee."

Holly muttered a few words that wouldn't have delighted her former Sunday-school teacher and looked around for Dr. Raymond. As she brushed past Maxine, the usually silent songbird said in a loud but weary tone, "Don't look so disgusted, Brooks. Good press is what pays all our salaries."

Holly glared at her, and Maxine shrugged. She had donned, for the occasion, a fringed white suede bolero with matching miniskirt, and her blouse and buckskin boots were decorated with enough elaborate Indian beadwork to stir the envy of Chief Sitting Bull's squaw. "It's part of being Lee's chick," she hissed. "He needs his publicity and he needs his friends. Can you dig it?"

Maxine's laughter followed Holly as she stormed her way across the room, jostling and being jostled by the increasingly noisier crowd. She made her way to where she saw Dr. Raymond standing beside Lee's wheelchair, and as she approached, Lee apparently saw her for the first time since she had entered the suite.

"And it's high time, luv!" he shouted. "Can't have a proper homecoming without my pet bird. Let her by, you types . . . this is favorite people."

Holly glanced from Lee's radiant face to that of the doctor, noting the latter's grim, almost accusing expression. Still shaken by the encounters with the press and with Maxine, she had to make an effort to stay calm. "Have you met Dr. Raymond, Lee? He was expecting to find you alone."

"I'm never alone," Lee sang out. The earlier fatigue lines were gone from his face; his smile vied with the flashing photo bulbs that illuminated his features every few seconds. "I've all *sorts* of friends, but there's only one true love. Gentlemen, this is Holly Brooks from Holly*wood*. C'mon over and give us a kiss, pet. Give these ink-stained vultures something to write about."

The reporters laughed, but they seized the bait avidly:

"Can we quote you as saying that you and Miss Brooks . . ."

82

"Where did you fall in love? Was it before or after your accident?"

"Are you planning to be married?"

"How about a shot of the two of you together? Miss Brooks, if you'd just lean over the chair with your arms around . . ."

It was bedlam all over again, and Holly was saved by the sudden exit of Glenn Raymond. He had said something about returning at a more logical time, but the words had been drowned out in the uproar caused by Lee's hint of a serious romance. As one of the press photographers took Holly's arm, urging her closer to the wheelchair, she said, "Excuse me . . . I've got to talk to the doctor," and jerked herself free.

She heard Lee calling to her, telling her to hurry back, as she sidestepped her way to the door. As she closed it behind her, she saw Dr. Raymond turning the corner, headed for the elevator. She caught up with him before the down car arrived.

"Dr. Raymond . . ."

He turned, eyeing her as though he had never seen Holly before.

"I'm terribly sorry you weren't able to . . . examine your patient. I had no idea . . . when I left Lee, he was —"

"I *did* examine him," the doctor said.

83

"But you couldn't —"

"It doesn't require an examining room or an armamentarium to determine that a man is under the influence of a drug."

"He can't be," Holly protested. "I haven't even been asked for a sleeping pill, let alone —"

"Under the influence of a drug," Dr. Raymond repeated firmly. "Stimulating drug of some kind. Not marijuana, although I caught a sniff of that unmistakable sweetish smoke in the room. I expect that can be attributed to some of the guests, and in any case, the effects wouldn't be as obvious. I'm not talking about a mild non-narcotic. Didn't you notice his eyes? Or that manic, effusive manner?"

Holly frowned. "You've never seen Lee close up before, Doctor. When he's surrounded by a crowd, when he's excited about something, he's always bursting with energy. Are you sure you aren't confusing an extremely dynamic personality with —"

"I'm *quite* sure." Dr. Raymond's tone had a razor-sharp edge. "I can't determine from such a cursory observation exactly what Mr. Watson is 'on.' Benzedrine, perhaps. Has he had access to barbiturates? Dr. Von Engel hasn't written a certificate, from the medication records I've seen."

"Certificate?"

"I believe you use the word 'prescription.' "

"No."

"Were there any changes in medications since Dr. Von Engel forwarded the case history?"

Holly thought for a moment. "He was taken completely off morphine. I don't know if the record —"

"I have that data, yes. I wish I could be certain it's been observed."

"I can assure you it *has* been," Holly said. She sensed a personally critical attitude on the doctor's part, as though he were questioning her dependability. "That applies to every drug you can name, except the sleeping pills and the pain pills I told you about earlier. And Lee hasn't had either of those since we left the hospital in Los Angeles."

One elevator car had come and gone during their discussion. Another set of pneumatic doors whined open now, but the doctor ignored the fact. "I don't know what we're dealing with. Cocaine, heroin, bennies — God help him, possibly morphine. When I can see Mr. Watson alone, I won't neglect looking for fresh needle marks, I assure you. In the meantime, I'm quite sure you should be able to determine where your patient is getting his certificates filled. Not at a chemist's shop, I'm quite certain. Incidentally, our chemist shops are your drug stores, I believe. Neither trades in narcotics. We like to think a patient under private care is afforded the same protection."

Holly bristled at the thick sarcasm. "Dr. Raymond, I told you I haven't provided my patient with any drugs. In the past forty-eight hours he hasn't required any. I've been Lee Watson's nurse since the moment he came out of surgery, and I've seen him through some agonizing periods . . . physical and emotional."

"Miss Brooks, I have no doubt that —"

"You're implying doubts, Doctor!" Holly flared. "I've even nursed my patient through drug-withdrawal symptoms, when Dr. Von Engel got concerned about a dependency on morphine. I can't appreciate your coming in at this late stage, glancing at a patient you know next to nothing about personally, and leaping to the conclusion that I've been negligent!"

"Are American nurses in the habit of haranguing the doctor in charge of a case?" Dr. Raymond's voice was infuriatingly

86

calm, an embarrassing contrast with Holly's rising shrillness. "Because, Miss Brooks, however late I may have come in on the case, the responsibility for this patient *has* been shifted to me, you know."

"That's why I think you ought to know about Dr. Von Engel's technique of treating the whole patient," Holly countered. "Lee needs the stimulation of his —"

"His friends. His career. You might want to acquaint yourself with my articles on the subject. I can't expect you to subscribe to British medical journals, but I can provide you with copies." Dr. Raymond's dark stare was devastating. "However strongly I may feel about the strain of that . . ." He gestured, indicating the still audible party scene around the corner. ". . . that madness I walked into, I'm conscious of its importance to this patient's morale. If I can prevent a patient from making a radical change in his life style after an amputation, I consider him well on the road to a healthy adjustment. I try to get a patient to face his new condition and carry on. Unfortunately, when a patient can't face his infirmity, can't carry on without blotting the handicap out of his consciousness with narcotics, I become concerned with *that* part of the whole patient. And I expect the nurse in charge to be equally concerned."

Fatigue and the unjustified attack broke Holly's last grip on self-control. "I don't know what you expect of me, Dr. Raymond! I know that I don't have to apologize for —"

"No apologies needed," he said tonelessly. "It shouldn't be too difficult to learn what your patient swallowed, sniffed, or injected this afternoon. You can't watch him every instant, of course. Still, I rather imagine that a young lady who, by morning, will be the envy of every teenager in the Western Hemisphere enjoys Mr. Watson's confidence. You might ask him what he's using. And what his source is."

Holly opened her mouth to register a protest. There was no reason for Dr. Raymond to assume that she was romantically linked with Lee Watson. Just because a few reporters jumped at a facetious remark by Lee . . .

But, then, Lee wasn't being facetious. He had talked to Holly seriously about being in love with her, about needing and wanting her. And she hadn't had the strength to discourage him. Not completely. Merely accepting this assignment, coming to London with him when there *were* other nurse-therapists available in his home country, had been an extension of hope for Lee.

Swiftly, Holly's mind reviewed exactly what Lee had said to the reporters, how they had reacted, how she had been too irritated to bother with a denial. And Lee was too shrewd to throw out a sensational tidbit to the press unless he *wanted* to see it in print. Heaven only knew how Bart Mitchell had embellished the story by now. Why? For publicity purposes? The suggested marriage of a romantic symbol like Lee could only have an adverse reaction from his dream-motivated female admirers. Until he was actually married, each could visualize herself as the miraculously Chosen One, each listened to his records in lonely seclusion or in the company of thousands of equally unrealistic young counterparts in a theater, dreaming the impossible dream. Lee was fully aware that his popularity rested, in part, on these forlorn reveries. He would shatter that image only if his decision was genuine, and he had not only failed to deny his serious interest in Holly, he had virtually announced it!

No wonder Glenn Raymond's attitude toward me has changed, Holly thought. During a two-hour-long conversation, she had talked about everything from Lee's likes and dislikes in food to his former doctor's anachronistic taste in clothing, without once hinting that Lee Watson had claimed to be in love with her. Whether or not the patient had confused other emotions with love (which Holly believed), a doctor concerned with Lee's psychological well-being as well as his physical health should have been advised.

Yet, later, after Glenn Raymond had parted from her without any reference to their dinner date, Holly suspected that his cool disapproval of her was not only professional. He had been interested in her; she could hardly deny that the attraction was mutual. Why wouldn't he be turned off by the abrupt "discovery" that she was Lee Watson's girl?

Long after she had talked Bart Mitchell into dispersing the gala welcoming party, helped Rajah get their exhausted charge to bed, and returned to her own room, Holly berated herself for letting the doctor leave with that twisted impression.

She lay across her bed, watching billows of fog obscure the lights of the city, reminding herself that she would see Glenn Raymond again, that there would be an opportunity to tell him the truth, another chance to rekindle a spark that had been excitingly close to love at first sight.

That situation could be remedied, Holly assured herself. The doctor's carping criticism was another matter. How could you encourage a hopeful relationship when a man attacked your integrity, when he imposed impossible demands upon you, questioned your professional ability without knowing how devotedly you had served a patient?

Holly's anger fought off the sleep she so desperately needed. But along with her fury with the injustice of Glenn Raymond's remarks, she was plagued by a nagging suspicion. *Lee had suddenly stopped asking for drugs. Today, instead, he had asked to see Maxine, and Maxine, who served no purpose with the Tree of Life, who was "expendable" a few weeks ago, but was now kept on at an exaggerated salary, Maxine had broken a track record to respond to Lee's summons!*

Enjoying Lee's "confidence" may have seemed to be a simple solution to his new doctor. Holly knew better. *Maxine.* Of course. How could I have been so stupid? Holly wondered. Yet, someone had to save Lee from himself.

Bart Mitchell. Bart, whose whole purpose in life was apparently serving the Tree of Life, being Lee's best friend. Tomorrow she would turn the problem over to Bart. Bart. Holly yawned. Bart, the promoter, the trouble-shooter, the man who was paid to make everything right . . . Bart would help.

SIX

"Don't blame yourself," Bart Mitchell said. "I'll tell the doc not to blame you, either."

He had taken the afternoon off from the busy Tree of Life office, located near the hotel and buzzing, during Holly's pre-dinner visit, with hectic activity. She hadn't realized that a virtual empire had developed around Lee's talents. Lee Watson guitars, Lee Watson apparel, recordings, concert bookings, posters, investments, and an unbelievable assortment of related enterprises were kept rolling under the squint-eyed promoter's supervision, yet he was trying to fulfill Lee's direction — that Holly should see and be given every opportunity to "fall in love with London."

During the past week, Bart had made an effort to introduce Holly to the attractions *he* considered important and "in." There had been a shopping tour along Carnaby Street, where Holly was encouraged to buy mod fashions that would "blend her into the scene," after which Bart dismissed Holly's interest in a visit to Kew Gardens,

Parliament, the Tower of London, and the celebrated Changing of the Guard at Buckingham Palace as "boringly touristy," and, following Lee's orders, introduced her to the inner social world to which "the Tree crowd" had access.

"Any Kansas City plumber's wife can scrounge about for an eighteenth-century silver crumb tray in the Portobello Road," Bart had said when Holly expressed a desire to visit the celebrated Saturday antique market. "Lee wants you to make the trendy scene."

"Trendy" meant sipping iced crab soup in a quaint restaurant in Chelsea, walking down flights of narrow steps to dark basement discotheques where deafening music blared and psychedelic lights flashed across a sea of jostling bodies. It meant being presented to theatrical celebrities at a pub off Berkeley Square, and taxiing from a French restaurant in the garishly lighted Soho district to a private party given by a currently popular artist who had managed to crowd such an enormous, if unhomogenous, mob of young sophisticates into his little red-brick studio along King's Road that there was barely room for his colorful guests to converse vertically without jabbing each other with their elbows.

Meeting the famous personalities, writers, actors, musical stars, and government bigwigs, had been a hurried, almost surrealistic experience for Holly. But the parties could have taken place anywhere, including Los Angeles, the only difference being that here, because she knew Lee Watson, she had access to the glittering celebrity world. Returning to the hotel, it had been difficult to answer Lee's eager question — "Did you enjoy yourself, luv?" — impossible to tell him that she would have preferred meeting people who worked in less glamorous fields, as she did; people with whom she felt comfortable. Or that she had actually looked forward to the "boringly touristy" attractions that had intrigued her in the guide books.

Rajah had been relieved, this evening, by an equally quiet young Irishman named Ian Boyd, leaving Holly free to let Bart Mitchell perform his duties as an escort. She had brought up, as she had been doing daily, the subject of Lee's possible access to narcotic drugs. This time, Bart hadn't been able to divert her attention and change the subject. Seated across the table from Holly in one of the chic, candlelit, and impossible-to-find dining hideaways that the "in" crowd made a point of finding, Bart toyed with his flan dessert and sighed. "You can't help Lee, old girl. That's the one fact of life all of us who admire him can't escape." Melancholy gray eyes met Holly's, communicating a pain she had never seen there before. "He's got to burn himself up in a hurry. That's *Lee*."

"Are you telling me that you know he's using drugs?" Holly demanded. "And that there's nothing you or anyone else can do about it?"

Bart didn't give her a direct answer. "He's a genius, Holly. He has compulsions you and I can't begin to understand. One of them is living as though there weren't any tomorrow."

"But he can be helped! With all Lee has to live for —"

"Ducks?" Bart's pinched face jutted forward and he peered at Holly over the rimless spectacles, looking more like a wizened old man than an under-thirty ball of fire.

Holly ignored the questioning tone, arguing, "I mean it, Bart. We don't just say he's got a compulsion to burn himself out and let it go at that. We try to —"

"*Ducks?* Have you ever tried to stop a hurricane? I used to try. Believe me. I love the type. I'd say 'e's like a brother to me, if I didn't detest my moneygrubbing shopkeeper of a brother. Lee . . ." Bart released a long sigh and set down his spoon, giving up interest in the food before him. "Lee is something else. You know? Like his clock's been set differently from yours and mine. You can't hope to understand him. You'd jolly well better forget about trying to change him. If he means a great deal to you, best to accept him as he is. Live with it. You can break your 'ead an' your 'eart trying to make 'im over. And what *right* do we 'ave, trying to change 'im?"

Holly made an exasperated sound. "I don't want to change him, Bart. I want him to go on making his music, developing that fantastic talent, seeing him well and happy instead of . . ." She let a shuddering motion express her thoughts.

"What do you know about 'well' or ' 'appy' in Lee's frame of reference? Oh, I used to think I did. Keep 'im straight. Do what I could to see that he didn't destroy 'imself." Bart sounded on the verge of tears. "What do I know about the insides of an artist? What compels 'im, what makes Lee able to do what I can only envy? I know 'e laughs harder, cries more pain. 'E feels . . . how do I say it? Feels with an intensity that makes me seem a shallow imitation of a human being by comparison. I don't any longer pretend that I know what's right for Lee."

"We know killing himself with morphine isn't going to help him," Holly insisted. "Let's not get abstract and evade the issue. It's that simple, Bart. If you care for the man, you've got to protect him from himself."

Bart's voice dropped to a solemn murmur. "Don't ever think you can, Holly. Once in a lifetime, you might . . . you just *might* meet a star-crossed spirit that can't be analyzed and pigeonholed and handled the way you might do with 'Arry Frisby, down the street, or your own brother. You can try. You can get your 'eart broken, too." He had been gazing absently at the flickering candle flame. Now Bart fixed Holly with a demanding stare. "Tell me something, stranger. Are you in love with 'im?"

Holly met the blinking gray eyes with her own. "No. No, I . . . care a great deal what happens to him, Bart. Maybe I even love him, after a fashion. But I'm not in love *with* Lee."

"That's good," Bart said, surprisingly. "I'm relieved to hear it."

"Why?"

"Because I like you. I know Lee needs

love. There's never goin' t' be enough, y'know. Deludes 'imself, sometimes, into thinking he can love someone back." Bart closed his eyes for a moment and then opened them to survey Holly's face with a look of infinite sadness. " 'E can't do it, dollybird. Might be the element that separates a great talent from the rest of us, I can't say. I *do* know, the only way to love the Watson is . . . take the way Maxine digs 'im. Expects nothing back. Any other way is to get your 'eart broken. So, you see, ducks, I'm glad you've escaped the curse. Don't like to see anybody get hurt."

Holly thanked him, and reminded Bart that not being in love with Lee didn't mean being completely free of his emotional hold on people. "I care what happens to him. I care a lot. And this drug thing . . . if it's true . . ."

"Assuming it is, what do you think any of us could do about it if we tried? Argue with him? Lock 'im in a cage?" Bart made a shrugging gesture. "Nobody ever stopped Lee from doing what he wanted to do. Most of what he's accomplished was done in spite of others. The people who told him to take a clerk's position and forget about music. The agents and club owners who wouldn't even listen to 'im.

The friends who warned 'im this or that was too chancy, too new to be accepted, too far out to catch the public fancy. Lee's always gone ahead and carved his own path through the jungle."

"You're talking about his successes," Holly pointed out. "What about —"

"What about trying to slow 'im down?" Bart released a short, bitter laugh. "Forget it! Accept 'im. That's all you can do." Bart's voice softened, and it seemed to Holly that he was pleading for her understanding when he said, "And don't be fooled by the cocksure preparations for this big free concert. Lee's turning out ideas and sounds and energy as though . . . as though there was a time limit hanging over 'im. That fantastic enthusiasm. That . . . complete self-assurance. Don't let it fool you, old girl. You're looking at a terrified man. Don't presume to know what Lee needs to keep going."

It was an argument for which Holly had no answer and one that she kept in mind during the weeks that followed, when the Tree of Life filled Lee's sumptuous hotel suite with an exhilarating new sound, when Lee, propped up in his bed or perched precariously on the edge of his wheelchair seat, coaxed a strangely soul-stirring music from his guitar, his voice ringing, pleading, laughing, bemoaning all the loneliness in the world or poking satirical fun at that same world's pompous blindness, but never merely singing; communicating with the deep wellsprings of emotion that human beings conceal from each other and that art reaches out to touch when even love fails.

Holly watched him with a kind of awe, seeing Lee's vitality as almost superhuman, his demands for perfection almost godlike. He would flatter or hurl curses at the other members of the group with equal gusto and for the same intended purpose. Once, dissatisfied with the blending of two instruments on a single chord, he ranted and shrieked, then spoke as softly as a gentle parent, forcing the others to repeat the measure until nerves were frayed, everyone was exhausted, and only respect or pity (or perhaps a combination of both) kept the musicians from quitting in anger. Ironically, when the effect Lee had wanted was finally achieved, he ripped up the "lead sheets" he had written for the new song, and declared that the number now sounded "wooden, over-rehearsed and unspontaneous." Ironically, too, when Desmond relieved the tension by giggling at the ludicrousness of the situation, and the others, more timidly, joined in, Lee's uproarious laughter led them all into a convulsion of hilarity that lasted for a full ten minutes.

Later, as the group members were leaving, Holly overheard Norb Sutliffe, the pony-tailed intellectual who played bass, sigh. Near the door, Holly asked, "Wear you out, did he?"

Her sympathetic question was rewarded with a poisonous glance. "He doesn't drive anybody harder than he drives himself. If you were a musician and you were *listening,* you'd know that being worn out by *him* is a privilege."

Rebuffed, Holly began to appreciate the stature of her patient, the superiority that permitted him to behave like a tyrant and get away with it. But still later, when she was alone with Lee and the room was suddenly silent, when she was forced to return him to the mundane world of dressings and therapeutic exercises, and when he abruptly caught her hand, clinging to it with unsteady fingers, eyes pressed shut, his breath resembling the gasping dry sobs that come when tears are depleted but the hurt that caused them remains, Holly knew that Bart Mitchell was right; that even gods can be terrified, for there is no direction left for them except down.

"You're not unhappy here, are you, luv? Bart's been seeing to it that you get out . . . see the old town?"

Holly gave her assurance that she was, indeed, happy. "Bart's been wonderful to me, taking time off to take me places."

"Wouldn't want you to leave," Lee said, his inflection telling her that he didn't really expect her to stay.

"I'm not leaving." *Now,* Holly thought. Face him with the question about drugs, tell him you refuse to stay unless he tells you the truth. She tried to approach the subject tactfully. "Not as long as I think my being here is serving some purpose. If you'll follow orders, cooperate with Dr. Raymond, tell us about any problem that —"

"Your *being* here," Lee broke in. "That's the purpose you serve. Simply being here." His grip tightened, pressing Holly's fingers together tightly. "I love you so awfully, it hurts, darling. I need you . . . more than you could possibly know." He sounded less tortured, almost matter-of-fact as he said abruptly, "The concert's not far off. I couldn't go on with it, if I didn't have you close by. Incidentally, has Bart shown you any of the advance publicity?"

Had Lee sensed that an unpleasant subject had been about to come up, and had he deftly avoided it? "There's been so much notice, the authorities are expecting problems in logistics. Traffic snarls, and all that."

"Yes, Bart said there's no need for promotion. He told me that just whispering the word to one teenaged girl would bring out a record-breaking crowd." Holly smiled. "Why not? You've drawn standing-room-only crowds when people had to pay to get in. And this is your first free concert."

"It'll be my first standing-room-only concert sitting down," Lee said tersely. Before Holly could think of words with which to end this self-pitying turn in the conversation, Lee brightened. "What I probably need is a booster. Read some of the publicity notices."

"I'm sure you'd enjoy them."

Rajah had come into the room, carrying one of the long-sleeved silk paisley pajama suits Lee had taken to wearing and a fresh set of underclothing. He murmured, "It is time for the bath, Mr. Watson." Holly decided to shelve the confrontation about drugs until a more convenient time.

Lee let go of her hand reluctantly. "When will you come back?" he asked.

"Soon as you've had your bath. Tell you what."

"Tell me."

"I'll have a tray sent up here and have my dinner with you."

"Beautiful."

Holly paused near the door. "I want a long talk with you, Lee. Something we . . . really have to discuss."

Perhaps Lee assumed that she was referring to their never-discussed "engagement," a vagary with which gossip columnists were having a field day. His charming smile flashed on. "I can't wait. Harv tells me *Mod Scene* ran a story about our wedding plans. Wouldn't you like to have the article handy during dinner? We ought to find out what we'll be wearing and where the ceremony takes place."

Lee was joking about the presumptuous fan magazine, of course, but there was no assurance that the subject of marriage to Holly was a joke to him. How often, since their arrival in England, Lee had repeated the sentiments Holly had just heard from him: *"I love you so awfully it hurts. I need you . . . I need you. Oh, Holly, how desperately I need you to restore my peace!"*

In spite of his outward confidence, Lee was frightened and bewildered; he was driven and lost. This was not the time to dash cold water over his hopes. What was needed here was a patient waiting game. After the concert (and there was no doubt in Holly's mind that it would be a smashing success), with his enormous ego bolstered, assured that his handicap would have no bearing on his career, Lee would probably forget all about his need for a nurse with whom he had little in common. They had shared the aftereffects of a tragic accident; apart from that, what other bond was there between them?

"I'll see if I can get a copy of *Mod Scene* in the foyer downstairs," Holly promised as she started out of the room.

"No need," Lee called after her. "I'm sure it's been dutifully pasted into Maxine's press-notice book." With an attempt at casual indifference that, somehow, failed to ring true, he added, "I'll have Rajah give her a jingle . . . have her bring it around in a bit."

Holly returned to her own quarters with the sensation of feeling a leaden weight in her stomach. Maxine again. Maxine, at a time when Lee's fantastic energy and enthusiasm had run low, like an unwound clockspring. He was depressed now, filled with self-doubt and a dread of being left alone by the one person who didn't depend on his success for her livelihood. Every other friend Lee had was dependent on him; did the king wonder how long he would be surrounded by his worshipful subjects if his talents failed him? And when the fear came over Lee, did a hasty call to Maxine provide him with the chemical reassurance his mind and body cried out for?

It couldn't go on. Holly's first thought was to call Bart. Bart Mitchell, the fixer-upper, whose whole life revolved around smoothing ruffled waters and making things right. But Bart had already expressed his opinion on the subject; there was nothing he could do, nor was he certain that anything should be done.

It was a medical problem, Holly reminded herself. Medical problems demanded the attention of a doctor. It wouldn't be easy, admitting to Glenn Raymond that he had been right and she had been wrong, especially since he had, during his daily visits to Lee's room, taken on a coldly professional attitude, barely acknowledging Holly's existence except to tell her he had more important matters to attend to than calling on someone who was always too busy for a thorough examination and a nurse who either had to be blind, or was consciously cooperating with a drug-addicted patient.

Holly had barely spoken to the doctor after that cutting inference. Was it her anger with him, or the devastating effect Glenn Raymond had on her, that made the telephone call now a trembling experience?

Holly reached him, after nerve-racking delays, at a nursing home for paraplegics. "I've got to talk to you, Doctor," she said after telling him who was calling.

There was a split-second pause. "I'm quite busy, Miss Brooks." Even the crisp, no-nonsense voice had a thrilling effect. "Is this an emergency?"

Holly considered the question for another micro-instant before saying, "Yes. Yes, I think it's a serious matter."

"You want me to see Mr. Watson at once, I expect. I might be able to get away in . . . perhaps twenty, twenty-five minutes. I can't possibly leave sooner, and I'm a full half hour's drive from your hotel. If it's a matter of . . . that is, if you have a situation you can't manage, I can get another physician over in a matter of minutes, I expect."

"No, I'd rather wait for you, Dr. Raymond. Could you ring me when you get here?"

"You aren't with the patient?" The doctor's voice rose slightly, his tone questioning.

"At the moment, no. I'll explain when you get here. And . . . I do appreciate it, Dr. Raymond."

He muttered a polite acknowledgment and rang off.

Within the hour, he was knocking at Holly's door, and then she was guiding him to one of the overstuffed chairs near a window that provided a spectacular view of the city. Ill at ease, Holly sat down in an identical chair opposite his, wishing her nervousness in Glenn Raymond's presence were not so obvious.

He had asked the professional question as they crossed the room: "Now, then, what seems to be the difficulty?"

Holly decided to be equally direct. "I think your first diagnosis was right."

"Oh? Really."

"I don't know what Lee . . . Mr. Watson's using, but I've been observing the symptoms you pointed out."

"Dilated pupils . . . what else? Does he act withdrawn?"

"No. No, he's never withdrawn," Holly

replied. "But there's a radical fluctuation in his moods. Part of it is his personality. That's what confused me; it's his nature, I think, to go from manic enthusiasm to a . . . sort of run-down, reflective state. Of course, I've only known Lee since his accident, but I gather from his closest friends that this was always his normal pattern."

"Yet you're convinced now that this is not the case?" Dr. Raymond was hardly disinterested, but his way of speaking, even the way he looked at Holly, was so impersonal that he may as well have been addressing the round oak tea table that separated them. "Explain the *specific* symptoms you've observed, please."

"For one thing, he hasn't let me rub his back or . . . for example, when I finally talked him into doing the prone push-up exercise, he's careful not to remove his shirt, something he always insisted upon doing in the hospital. Because he said it got in his way. The fabric bunched up under him, or there were buttons that pressed against his chest and he complained about that. He doesn't now. And I know the long-sleeved shirts or those kimono-like pajamas he's been wearing only get in his way when he plays the guitar."

"You're saying that he hasn't let you see

his arms." Dr. Raymond nodded gravely. "He's also found excuses to put me off. You recall my having to slip the stethoscope down the neck of his shirt . . . that satin affair that zips down the back. Used every possible ploy to avoid the simple process of slipping it off. Yes." The doctor was thoughtfully silent for a moment. "It's rather painfully apparent that we aren't talking about barbiturates, for example. Not that this wouldn't be a matter of concern."

"It could be something like that," Holly offered. Instinct and the circumstances told her otherwise.

"I'm afraid this patient is concealing fresh needle marks," Dr. Raymond said bluntly. "He's hooked on morphine."

Holly shuddered inwardly. "Dr. Von Engel was worried about something like this. I . . . think he blamed himself."

Whatever Glenn Raymond thought about the American doctor's responsibility in the case, ethics and discretion kept him from making a comment. He mumbled, to himself, something about "a predisposition" and got up from his chair. With his back turned to Holly, he stared down at the scene below. The last glow from the setting sun reflected from the Thames, an orange-pink ribbon woven through the city. It was a remarkably clear evening, for London, and Holly almost missed the fog. It belonged, somehow. Today's bright sunlight had seemed, like herself, a misplaced visitor from Los Angeles.

Holly let the idle thoughts occupy her mind, letting Dr. Raymond ponder the problem undisturbed. Only a few moments elapsed before he turned, his dark, serious eyes probing Holly's, as though he had just noticed her presence. "There's only one course open, naturally. Get the patient into a proper institution. I can recommend several that provide every facility. One can't guarantee results. So much depends upon the patient's degree of addiction, his determination to be cured, his metabolism, his emotional state."

"I don't think anyone could even approach Lee with the idea of going into . . . an institution," Holly said.

"I'm not talking about a penal institution," the doctor said irritably. "We take a more humane, and, I think, more realistic attitude toward drug addiction in this country than you do in yours. In England, the addict is a victim, not a criminal. His problem is an illness, not an offense. The addict's only threat to society, you know, is not his use of the drug but his inability to afford or obtain something his body *must* have, just as it can't exist without oxygen."

"I'd heard something about clinics," Holly recalled. "Where an addict can get a shot when he needs it."

"Legally. Under proper supervision. A registered case." Dr. Raymond's handsome face creased in an expression of incredulousness. "I've never understood the American thinking on the subject. What alternatives do you leave these miserable creatures *except* to turn to theft, prostitution, even murder?" The doctor grew impatient with the discussion, suddenly. "I didn't tear myself away from a heavy caseload of patients to lecture on America's medieval approach to a medical problem. Mr. Watson, being wealthy, won't have to resort to robbing petrol stations, certainly. I'm not a prosecutor. As a doctor, for the sake of this patient's health, I have the responsibility of urging him to submit to treatment. Admittedly chancy treatment; complete cures, where the patient stays off morphine permanently, aren't as common as one might wish. Still, with some of the new drugs that make withdrawal less traumatic, with psychological help, and with substitutes that allay the craving . . ."

"Lee couldn't go back into a hospital now," Holly said. "He'd be completely shattered."

"He isn't going to improve his condition going his present course," the doctor predicted.

"If we could just wait until this big concert's behind him. You can't imagine what it means to him . . . a chance to prove that he isn't a useless, unwanted cripple."

"I keep having to remind you," Dr. Raymond said in a caustic tone, "that I am *quite* able to understand a patient's psychological needs. I shouldn't have to remind you that every day that goes by commits Mr. Watson more deeply to his physical need for a dangerous drug. I'm not even certain that anxiety about this public performance hasn't precipitated the problem we're faced with."

Holly thought about it for a moment and reluctantly admitted that this was true. "What I *do* know is that this concert has given Lee a reason for living. If we take that away from him . . ."

"Exactly what *do* you propose?" There was no mistaking the doctor's annoyance with her now. "After the concert there will be a recording session, and after the album is recorded, his 'reason for living' will be a

114

tour of the Continent or Australia or a return trip to the United States. Meanwhile, the anxiety and the addiction will be completely out of hand."

Holly rose to her feet, sick at the thought of approaching Lee with the doctor's program. "I wouldn't know how to . . ."

"You aren't being charged with the responsibility for telling *my* patient what *I* think must be done."

Holly returned the doctor's hostile glare. What made him so smug and unpleasant? More than that, what had made her think that she could possibly fall in love with this dictatorial, waspish man? For she *had* sensed herself falling in love with him, Holly remembered. A short time ago, just knowing that he stood outside her door had set her heart pounding like a tom-tom. Yet, during their initial meeting, he had given her a totally different impression. And he had visited Lee Watson in Holly's presence often enough to know that there was no genuine romance between them. What had happened to the warm rapport that had existed the first time they met?

It didn't matter. He was a blunt, unsympathetic person; his cold-turkey approach, when he talked to Lee, might have devastating results. "On second thought," Holly said, "it might be better if I talked to Lee."

"I should think so. Yes," the doctor agreed. "It's a highly sensitive matter and I don't delude myself that it will be easy to . . . even to broach the idea, to say nothing of implementing it. Sometimes impersonal medical advice is more easily accepted than urging from, say, a relative. Conversely, a delicate matter should be entrusted to someone who is very close to the patient."

"Well, Lee knows I've seen him through some rough periods. I think he trusts me. But he's unpredictable and . . . I'm not really that close to him."

"One of my patients, an elderly lady who was crippled during the Blitz, assures me that you are," Dr. Raymond said. He wore an expression that could only be described as snide.

"I don't know any of your patients, except Lee Watson," Holly said curtly. "I'm sure none of them knows me."

"Poor Mrs. Graves lives vicariously," the doctor said with an exaggerated patience. "She can tell you about the current romantic state of every movie or singing star on both sides of the Atlantic. Naturally, when she learned that Mr. Watson is my patient, she wanted to know all about the 'dear little American nurse who'd saved his life, the one he's going to marry.' "

"But that's not —"

"She let me see her sources of information. I expect congratulations are in order."

"Those cheap gossip magazines! They invent —"

"So I'm confident that if anyone can reach Mr. Watson, you should be able to do it," Dr. Raymond said, ignoring Holly's feeble protest. It was as though he hadn't heard her, and perhaps he hadn't, because his mind was concentrated on the problem that had brought him to the hotel. "If you want to bring pressure to back you up, you might convince Mr. Watson that unless he submits to treatment, neither I, nor any other physician, can assume responsibility for his well-being. There isn't much I can do unless Mr. Watson wants to help himself. And there are simply too many people in need of help, people who *want* to be cured, for me to devote time to a hopeless case." The doctor glanced at his watch. "I left a number of them waiting. You'll excuse me, Miss Brooks, I'm sure."

His brusque, hurried manner told Holly that she had detained Glenn Raymond long enough. He had responded to her call, given his opinion, and there was nothing more to say. When he closed the door behind him, Holly knew of two reasons, one professional and the other personal, why he might never return.

SEVEN

It was impossible to raise the subject that evening. Holly had expected to set down a firm but sympathetic ultimatum after the quiet dinner hour with Lee. Instead, when she stepped into the suite, it was a bedlam of agents, critics, record-company executives, and assorted hangers-on who had been invited by Bart for a preview of the forthcoming free concert.

Lee was too immersed in leading the Tree of Life in their "new sound" to apologize to Holly for the change in plans. Afterward, when the din and the praise were finally ended, he was both too exhausted and too overstimulated for a serious discussion of anything but how enthusiastically his new songs and his radically different arrangements had been received.

While waiters cleared the smoke-filled suite of empty glasses and hors d'oeuvre trays, Bart lingered behind the other "in" people to rave, "It's going to be like you never 'ad a scene before, Lee! Like this is a whole new thing, better than ever before!

Weren't they fab, Holly? Wasn't our boy something else?"

"It was very exciting," Holly admitted. "I'm not sure this much strain is good for Lee."

Rajah was in the process of wheeling Lee to his bed. "The bass is too persistent in the 'Violet Star' piece," Lee said. "I've called a two-o'clock rehearsal . . . see if I can get Norb to understand this is an ethereal experience, not a Mau Mau uprising."

"It could be more subtle, all round," Bart agreed. "I don't know, chum. It got to me. Good vibes, you know."

"It's not right." Lee was being lifted into his bed by his powerful, sphinx-like orderly, his mind completely consumed by a critical analysis of the night's performance. "My fault, actually. I was coming on like a . . . starving soul singer auditioning for a gig in Las Vegas. This is a delicate mood thing, Bartie."

After he was eased against the pillows, Lee said abruptly, "I think *any* dude singing those lyrics is going to make it too heavy. It's a feminine sort of thing . . . soft air and misty-colored love dreams. I think it should be sung by a bird."

Bart could be adamant in an argument about business details, but he never questioned Lee's musical judgment. "Could Maxine 'andle it?"

Lee didn't hesitate. "She's a *bit* tinny, but her voice has a good quality. What I want is a thin sound. Eternal woman wailing from a violet star five million miles off in space. Part of it would have to be a creative engineering job. Tell Lloyd and that other chap from the recording studio — what's his name, Korbel — I'd like a word with them."

"Morning all right?" Bart asked, slipping a leather-covered notebook from his jacket and jotting a note to himself.

"No, I'll have lost it by morning. It's in my head now and I won't be able to sleep if it isn't set."

Bart made a shrugging gesture at Holly, as if to say, "I know you don't approve, but what can I do?"

"Get them to come around tonight. And tell what's *her* name, — Minnehaha — I want to see her right away."

Holly felt her insides tighten. It was the same routine all over again; Lee throwing himself into his music, wearing himself out mentally, physically, emotionally. Then the quiet period when the music ended and he came face to face with himself in the silence, his mind free to think, his heart left alone to feel. It was this time when the fear swept over him, when the full knowledge of his loss assailed his consciousness. But there was a way to block out the pain. Maxine. He might, cleverly, dismiss her importance to him by calling her an absurd name, but there was nothing light about the summons. Maxine would bring him the saving grace of oblivion from reality.

An almost irrational anger swept over Holly. The girl knew what the result would be. Like a nurse who administers a pain-relieving hypo. Maxine might think of herself as a good Samaritan when she answered Lee's calls. She slept away the mornings, sometimes shopped in Carnaby Street in the early afternoon; usually sat, looking like an inanimate object, in a corner of the room during Tree of Life rehearsals. But always, Holly had observed, *always,* Maxine was in her room down the hall after sunset, fulfilling her single function, waiting for the pretext Lee would use to send for her. *Didn't she know what she was doing?*

Losing her temper would only alienate Lee and compound a critical situation. Making an effort to sound casual, Holly asked, "Are you sure it won't wait until morning, Lee? You've worked hard enough for one day. If you're too charged up to sleep, Bart and I will stay. We'll talk . . . maybe listen to the tapes you made tonight."

"I don't want to be babied," Lee snapped. "I know my own capacity for work. I know what I can do . . . what I've *got* to do, and when it's got to be done."

Bart raised a pacifying hand. "Holly isn't trying to interfere, chum. It's just that she doesn't want you worn out before the concert."

"There isn't going to *be* a concert if I don't get the sound I'm after." Lee reached out for a glass of water on the night table, making a painful grimace at the stretching motion. The glass was still out of his reach, and both Rajah and Holly moved forward to get it for him. *"I'm not going to be treated like a helpless cripple!"* he cried out.

Rajah stepped back, and Holly froze in her tracks. They were quiet, and only the sound of Lee's audible breathing was heard in the room while he turned over on his side, stretching his arm as far as possible. There was a terrible moment when he tried to get leverage by pushing himself with his leg and found it useless, when it seemed that his fingers would not be able to encircle the water glass, and his frustration would be total. Then he managed to grasp the half-filled glass. There was a collective sigh of relief as Lee pulled it to his lips, balancing himself precariously as he took one sip, proving that a drink of water had not been his objective at all. Then he held the glass out for Rajah to take, as if to say, "I've proved I'm not helpless. Here . . . this is what I'm paying you to do."

As he resettled himself in position on the bed, Lee was no longer belligerent. "I know I haven't had proper time for you, Holly," he said. Rajah made one of his discreet exits to another part of the suite. Bart, notebook still in hand, edged toward the door, not sure whether or not his presence was wanted. Apparently it still was. "Tell you what, Bart. Arrange for a limousine to take us out to Kent. Holly hasn't had a glimpse of the country, and I want her to see our future home."

Before Holly could say a word, Bart added another note to his bulging list of things to be done, saying, "When would you say, Lee? I've 'ad word the plumbers are finished piping in the sauna. Dining room's been redone, but the carpenter tells me he'll need another two weeks on the studio."

"Tell him he's got until day after tomorrow," Lee ordered.

"Oh, come off it, Lee. They can't possibly —"

"He can put more men on it. Acoustical tile's no big hangup. I could swing myself up a pulley and hammer up the ceiling myself. At least I don't have to worry about falling and breaking my leg." In a matter of seconds, Lee had run the gamut from considerate host to peevish boy to dictatorial tyrant to temperamental star. Now he was all charm again, smiling at his grim joke and saying to Holly, "It's a cushy place, luv. You can change whatever you don't like indoors, but I know you'll be mad for the grounds. Lawn's been thick as a mattress for nearly two hundred years. Green as a billiard table. Takes four gardeners just to keep the flower beds in trim. Oh, and a lovely pond to swim in. Sylvan. Only word to describe it; sylvan. You'll have to help me decide between keeping swans and installing a springboard. A stable, too. And all sorts of woody places to ride."

Holly fought to keep tears from welling in her eyes. In another second, Lee's excitement about the country manor he had bought prior to his trip to the States would end in a stabbing awareness: he would never dive from a springboard, swim in a

125

sylvan pond, or ride the woody trails on a favorite mount.

Holly didn't give him a chance to be jolted by the realization. "I'd love to see it," she said. "Will you have time, do you think? Before the concert?"

"We'll make time," Lee told her. He was every inch the executive in command now. "Bartie'll get us whisked from the underground garage here and we'll be in the country before the Watson-maniacs know it. No mob scene. Just a quiet drive and . . ."

"Lee?" He had sighed and closed his eyes. Holly exchanged a concerned glance with Bart. Looking at Lee closely, she whispered, "I think he wants to rest."

They waited for a few more seconds, Holly watching Lee's face and concluding that he wasn't really asleep. His frayed nerves, and perhaps the sudden collapse of a dream that he had started to describe, had become intolerable and Lee had chosen to black out the entire scene. It was time to leave him alone.

Holly talked with Bart Mitchell for a short time in the corridor, reporting to him what Lee's doctor had said, and deciding, after a series of evasions and subject changes, that Bart considered himself powerless to do anything about the situation. Even Holly's suggestion, that Lee's drug supply be cut off at its source, brought a hopeless reaction from the pinch-faced manager. "What makes you think Lee would let us get rid of Maxine? Especially now that he's found a use for her with the group? And once you've sent 'er packing, what do you think's going to hold Lee together, peppermint drops? Face it, ducks. If 'e's hooked, as you seem to think, booting Maxine out of the picture won't do anything but stir up a row."

"Are you telling me there's absolutely nothing we can do?" Holly demanded.

She expected Bart to offer an alternative, or, at least, to suggest stalling off any drastic moves until after the concert. Instead, Bart peered at her through his odd spectacles, nodded his head slowly and meaningfully, and said, "That's a possibility you might have to consider, old girl. Maybe you're out of your element. You aren't dealing with patient number two-ought-six in your tidy little hospital at home. You took on Lee Watson. Be advised, ducks. Lee is always going to be Lee."

It was an unsatisfactory, senseless conclusion to a discussion from which Holly had hoped to gain Bart's cooperation. From Glenn Raymond she had gotten an impossibly harsh solution, one that threatened to destroy Lee's principal reason for going on. From Bart she had gotten nothing but this hopeless evasion, as though Lee's admittedly strong personality placed him beyond human reach. The others?

Holly reviewed, in her mind, the vast army of Lee's friends and followers. They were exactly that — followers. Sycophants, worshippers, awed by their leader's strength, and too unperceptive to see his weakness, too concerned with staying on the gravy train to risk standing up to an engineer who had gone off the track.

No one else, then. And Lee had placed love and trust in Holly, clung to her, seeking her strength, admitting to her in those despondent moments that he needed the help of someone stronger than he. Finding a solution was a duty now, a moral responsibility. Whatever was done to save Lee had to be done quickly, and it had to be done, Holly decided, by herself alone.

She was too incensed, too overwhelmed with a sense of urgency and righteousness, to consider anything but the first drastic plan that leaped into her mind: *Stop*

Maxine, eliminate her from the picture. Lee would be cut off from his drug supply. Chances were that he was not so far gone that sedatives and liberal doses of love would not see him through the black period of withdrawal. She had nursed him through the same agony once before, had she not? It was a heavy burden to assume, but the reward of salvaging a gifted human being made the responsibility welcome.

Holly had only one momentary qualm, recognizing the depth of her ignorance about narcotics. For a frightened second or two she acknowledged to herself that she would be attempting a cure without understanding the disease. What was Lee taking? How could she provide an antidote without knowing the nature of the poison? More significant: if a counteracting or weaning drug substitute was necessary, only a doctor could tell her what it was; only an M.D. could prescribe what was needed.

That brief self-questioning was too unpleasant to face, for it led to a more serious prickling of the conscience; if she acted alone, she would be committing an unforgivable breach of ethics; she would be a nurse who was not only ignoring a doctor's instructions, but actually defying them, proceeding contrary to his orders.

Holly didn't let herself explore the possible repercussions. All heroic acts were acts of defiance, were they not? In the entire history of the world, and that included the medical world, no progress would have been made if people with bold ideas had dwelt too long on the consequences of a failure. Lee needed help. No one else cared enough to make the necessary move, no one else understood him enough to make the right move. She recalled the depth of Lee's anguish in those first days, when the pain of what had happened to him had been almost unendurable. She had guided him through that dark and twisted corridor once before. I can do it again, Holly assured herself. She went to sleep that night almost believing her own words.

EIGHT

Holly's confidence in her plan wavered again, but only for an instant, when her vigil was rewarded the next evening.

She had parted from Lee under what were now familiar circumstances. He had worked feverishly with the other members of his group all afternoon. Between rehearsals there had been press interviews, visits from a disc jockey, an electronic engineer who had perfected some improvement in electrical guitar amplifiers, the Tree of Life's equipment manager, and a delegation from the Associated Lee Watson Fan Clubs of Manchester. Gracious, witty, energetic, Lee had charmed his callers and exhausted his fellow musicians. When Rajah and Holly had ushered the last of these from his suite, he had all but collapsed in his wheelchair. Inevitably, before Holly had completed her now major nursing duties (Lee was obviously too worn out to consider even the simplest exercises), he found an excuse to summon Maxine.

"Desmond submitted an arrangement of 'Violet Star' that I like better than my own. Less gimmicky. Princess Morning Star can handle the simple melodic thread, I think, if she doesn't have to fight that heavy acoustical trip I had backing her."

Why the elaborate explanation, when Lee never wasted time discussing such technicalities with non-musicians? Why, for that matter, was it necessary to mention Maxine at all, when he could simply have waited for Holly to leave the room and then summoned "Princess Morning Star" by telephone?

Always that derogatory reference to Maxine's mode of dress, as though he wanted to make clear that he was not overly fond of the girl! It was as though he were *trying* to tell Holly that Maxine was of no personal interest to him, that she served another, unmentionable purpose. But *why?*

"I think I'll have the bird run through it once before I konk out," Lee said. (Was he only feigning that exhausted yawn? His attempt to sound casual was disastrous. Was that, too, deliberate? Why?)

Because he wants me to know his reason for calling Maxine, Holly concluded. It's his way of telling me what's wrong; Lee's indirect way of asking for my help, like the compulsive murderer who leaves clues for the police, begging to be stopped.

Armed with this further justification, Holly returned to her room and waited behind her slightly opened door, watching for Maxine. It was, as Holly expected an extremely brief waiting period, not long enough for her to develop second thoughts about the step she was taking. Yet, as she peered out to see Maxine's unusually brisk stride up the corridor, Holly felt a sudden panic. How did you approach someone like this? What did you say? And what if — terrifying thought, unpardonable! blunder — what if your suspicions were wrong?

Holly steeled herself against that flimsy possibility. As Maxine approached the door across the hall, Holly stepped out of her room and said, "Maxine?"

The girl whipped around, the fringe of her buckskin vest and skirt whirling like a ballet costume. She was plainly startled, but she said nothing, her expression more challenging than challenged.

Holly closed the short distance between them, nodding at the beaded suede Indian pouch Maxine always carried with her. "I'd like whatever you're taking in to Lee, please."

Maxine's pretense of innocence was betrayed by a rush of color to her face. Still, her dark, heavily mascaraed eyes flashed their normal hostility. "What*ever* can you be talking about, Miss Brooks?"

Holly met the now insolent stare. Quietly, trying to keep her voice from quavering (for there was no turning back now!), she said, "You and I both know what we're talking about, Maxine. We're both concerned with Lee's well-being. I don't question your motive in supplying him with drugs. The difference between us is that I'm responsible for that well-being. My interest is that of a professional nurse."

Maxine smirked. "I say! We do throw our qualifications around, don't we?" She brushed a wisp of long black hair from her forehead, smoothing it behind the beaded headband. Holly noticed that she held tightly to the strings of the long pouch. "If you have a complaint to register, I suggest you make it to Lee." A contemptuous half-smile curled up one corner of her mouth. "Or have you tried that, Nurse?"

Maxine's self-possessed response, now that the first flush of embarrassment had subsided, was unnerving. Holly straightened her shoulders, as though towering over Maxine's short stature would add strength to her argument. "We're talking about an extremely dangerous situation. I don't think there's any need to play games. May I have what I asked for?"

It was weakening not to be able to specify what was wanted. Perhaps Maxine caught this from Holly's unspecific request. She used it to her advantage. "You might tell me exactly what it is that you want, luv. I'm a singer, you know, not a psychic."

Holly's patience broke before her nerve. "I don't have time to play games, Maxine! You know what I'm talking about. Furthermore, you ought to know the risk you're taking in providing Lee with drugs."

Maxine reverted to type, clamming up, letting her face assume the vapid, faraway expression that always made you think she had removed herself from the scene.

"You're not just jeopardizing your own freedom," Holly persisted. The threat of a possible jail sentence failed to evoke any response. Holly appealed to the girl's single, obsessive emotion: "You're exposing Lee to a hell on earth. You don't understand his physical or nervous condition. The smallest overdose of . . ." Again it was necessary to water down her attack; to name a specific drug might reveal her ignorance. She pretended that the interruption was deliberate, looking down the corridor as if she were worried about being overheard. ". . . the wrong dosage of *any* kind of drug, even the drugs prescribed for him, could be fatal. Lee's had a tremendous shock to his system. I . . . I know you mean well. You're trying to do what's asked of you, probably against your own better judgment. But I'm sure that if you understand what you're doing to Lee . . . that you might be responsible for killing him . . ."

Holly let the shocking suggestion hang in midair. Did she only imagine it, or was there a subtle flicker of fear in those black-encrusted eyes? Fear, or perhaps . . . was it compassion? Holly had never doubted that the girl loved Lee. Only an insanely devoted person, and a masochistic one, at that, would tolerate Lee's alternate neglect, ridicule, and demands.

Maxine was impervious to threats of legal action; if she cared at all about herself she would have parted company with Lee Watson long ago. But the thought of hurting the object of her blind, slavish love . . . that was another matter. Holly pursued this softer line of persuasion, taking a few liberties with the truth to hammer her point home. "Dr. Raymond took blood samples this morning. He says that unless Lee —"

"Miss Brooks?"

Maxine's toneless, sighing voice saved Holly from embellishing the already serious situation with a dramatic lie. The girl was gazing at her with a strangely world-weary expression, as though she had seen and heard and experienced all there was to be seen and heard and experienced, and displays of callow ignorance affected her with exasperating boredom.

"*Nurse?*" Maxine pronounced the word the way Lee pronounced his good-humored but derisive Indian names for her. "Has it ever occurred to your smug little antiseptic brain that I know considerably more about the two subjects at hand than you do?"

Holly frowned, feeling the superiority of her height a small comfort. The tiny ersatz Apache maiden seemed to be towering over her now, her legs steady where Holly's had started to tremble, her voice a calm drone in contrast to Holly's emotion-charged tremolo. "I rather doubt that, but —"

"Drugs," Maxine said in an almost caressing purr. "I doubt that you'd know a vial of reds from a packet of snow. You probably think speed is something the bobbies control with the whistles about their necks. You probably think hash is a corned-beef dish and smack is something lovers do in the back row at a cinema."

The snide exaggerations weren't far from being true. Holly's formal schooling in pharmaceutics hadn't included slang terms for narcotics, nor, more significantly, the symptoms they produced and the therapy needed for their withdrawal. Holly made an attempt to save face. "I don't use the jargon you learned from dealing with pushers, no. But I know —"

"The *second* thing you don't know," Maxine went on in that colorless zombie tone of hers, "the *important* thing you don't know is your patient."

"And you do!" Holly challenged.

"Enough to be able to tell you that if you don't step out of my way in another second, he'll have Rajah out here looking for me. I'm never late, you know. Morning and evening, with or without a call from Lee, I'm never late, Nurse."

Holly swallowed down a shocked gasp. Mornings, too! With or without a call! Then Lee *had* been letting her know about the contacts with Maxine for a reason. He had been crying out, *"I can't stop myself. Stop me!"*

"Does that amaze you?" The heavy black

lashes blinked over Maxine's wide-staring eyes. "What did you expect, Nurse? You introduced Lee to the heavy goody. Your damn Yank pill-pusher laid it on him. Go back home and live with it! I'd have more feeling for a mongrel in the street."

Holly felt the color rising in her own face. Just or unjust, Maxine's accusation held the seeds of another truth. "You don't understand," she started.

"No, it's *you* doesn't understand," Maxine corrected. Her voice was bare of inflection, as flat and unwavering as her stare. "Now, you can have your choice, Miss B. Either you let me by or you call your bloomin' law to arrest me. In both cases, Lee's going to know what you're up to. Because, y'know, I'm going to tell him. Now, personally, or I'll ring him from my cell. It doesn't matter. He's going to know what you've done to him."

"But I want to help him!" Holly pleaded. "Why can't you understand?"

"*You* won't understand until an hour or two from now, when he's writhing in a cold sweat. When you can't stop the chills or the violent nausea or the racking cramps and diarrhea. Oh, look horrified, Nurse. Never've seen it before, have you? Well, I have, and I don't want to see it again!"

"You're only prolonging the agony!" Holly cried. "If we can stop the addiction before it grows —"

"You can 'cure' him," Maxine finished. Her voice held its monotone, though somehow it conveyed a scathing sarcasm. "Of course you can, medical genius. Call me when you're ready to give up. Before you hop your jet, leaving the wreckage behind you, call me, Florence Nightingale. Whenever, wherever Lee needs me, I'll be there."

"Pushing him over the brink!" Holly spat out. She was suddenly infuriated with this blank-staring creature who had ridiculed her profession, thrown vile accusations at a doctor she hadn't even met, and shaken Holly's confidence and conscience with a false impression. Maxine only *sounded* as though she knew what she was talking about. For a moment, Holly had confused the girl's superior attitude with knowledge. What did she know? *That a miserable man would permit her to stay around as long as she helped him along the road to hopeless drug addiction!*

Arguing with Maxine was not only debasing, it was a waste of time. Holly's fury with her exploded. "You aren't going to go on destroying Lee!" She made a lunging motion, as if to grab the suede pouch.

Maxine swung the bag behind her back to protect it. In the same instant, her free hand grabbed at Holly's hair, giving it a vicious yank.

It happened too fast for Holly to know whether she had struck out at Maxine to break her painful hold, or if Maxine, letting go of Holly's hair, had clawed at her face. There was no time for thought. There were only the two of them, breathing hard, releasing the grunts and panting sounds of animals locked in mindless combat, clumsily and blindly assailing each other with fists and nails as they wrestled for the pouch.

Miraculously, the disturbance was not heard inside Lee's quarters, and it was probably not the noise that attracted Bart Mitchell. He may have been leaving his room only to cross the hall for a confab with someone on the Tree of Life staff. His appearance wasn't noticed until Holly heard his hushed protest: "I say, what *is* this? Stop that, the two of you!"

As Bart shoved his small body between the two girls, attempting to separate them with outstretched arms, Holly managed to grab the suede bag. A violent tug from Maxine broke the frayed leather thong that

141

served as a handle and drawstring. Bart's shoving motion, which sent Maxine tumbling backward against a wall, was accompanied by a loud thud as the open pouch went flying in the opposite direction, spilling its contents.

Maxine leaned back against the wall, her long hair disheveled, gasping for breath. Equally breathless, her legs threatening to collapse under her, Holly stepped back. Both of them could only stare as Bart leaned over to pick up a bent spoon that had been thrown from the bag, and then a small plastic vial. He glanced up at Holly, his expression one of sorrow rather than shock. He retrieved the open pouch from the floor next, his hand extracting a hypodermic syringe that gleamed under the ceiling light like some evil entity with a life of its own. Bart tossed it back, along with the rest of the equipment, letting a mournful sigh speak for him.

Shaken, and ashamed of having reduced herself to a brawling level, Holly fought against fainting. She had suspected morphine or heroin, yet the conclusive sight of that hypodermic needle had carried the impact of a crashing blow to her stomach.

The silence probably lasted no more than a few seconds, yet it seemed that a long time had passed before Bart said, "Rather sorry prize to be fighting over." He turned to Maxine, who still hadn't recovered her composure. "Afraid that knocks it, old girl. Can't go on with it, you know. Exposure would ruin Lee and everyone else along with him."

"You . . . knew," Maxine managed to say. She spoke in a puffing, barely audible murmur, thick with contempt. "You knew, Bartie. You looked aside, is all you did."

"Can't very well look aside now, can I?" Bart leveled a stare at the girl, a stern look that was not devoid of tenderness. "You can't serve this purpose any longer, Maxine. I 'ope you'll make a graceful exit. You know? Like, you can't win 'em all. I shouldn't think you'd want me to . . . do my civic duty."

A moment ago, Holly had been furious with Maxine. Now, seeing the girl's beaten look, knowing that Maxine would separate herself from Lee forever before she would expose him to a drug scandal, Holly could only pity her.

Although her universe lay in ruins, Maxine remained dry-eyed and stoic. Her lips trembled, but there was neither venom nor self-pity in her dark, grotesquely painted eyes. By the light of her distorted

143

reasoning, she should have felt a violent loathing for Holly. If she did, it was not evident, possibly because her defeat was too devastatingly complete. She stepped away from the support of the wall, the fingers of one hand making a futile attempt to straighten the Indian headband which drooped askew over her forehead like the halo of a tipsy angel. She made a slow, shrugging motion with one shoulder, and started off, not in the direction of her room, but down the corridor toward the elevators.

"I'll write out a check," Bart said. He was not untouched; it was like seeing someone dying before your eyes. "Time you get back to your room to pack, I'll have a check covering the balance of your contract . . ."

Maxine wasn't listening. And there was something in her stride that told Holly she wouldn't come back for her possessions, or the money that was due her. Saying goodbye to Lee would have been unbearable torture. What else of value could she possibly be leaving behind? A bulging scrapbook, a futile dream. Her reason for being. Holly swallowed hard, fighting an urge to run after the incongruously dressed little imitation Indian, to tell

Maxine that she was sorry.

Halfway between Lee's door and the corner which she would turn on her way to the elevator well, Maxine stopped and turned around. Even at that distance, her black stare bored into Holly's eyes. Holly saw her lips move, as though Maxine were trying to form words. What did she want to say? "Tell Lee I love him? Be kind to him — don't let him suffer too long"? Or, simply, "God help you through the ordeal ahead"? These may have been romantic phrases, projected from the depth of Holly's deep sympathy for the girl. Maxine might have paused to hurl back an angry tirade, a string of curses. Whatever her intention, the words didn't come. For a terrible moment, Maxine stood motionless, her mouth twisting in an effort to say whatever remained to be said. Then she flung herself around, whirling the buckskin fringe, hurrying down the corridor. By the time Maxine rounded the corner, she was running.

Nine

"Good luck," Bart Mitchell had said. "I'll be in my room when you need me, duckie."

He hadn't said "if." Bart had given Holly a long, melancholy look and said "when." When Lee would demand to see him, furious about Maxine's dismissal? When Holly could no longer manage a drug-deprived addict alone?

"I'll tell him the truth," Holly had assured Bart. "I won't even have to tell him you were involved. Just leave word at the switchboard. No incoming calls to Lee. And no outgoing calls, for that matter. Yes, that's even more important. Have them . . . disconnect Lee's line."

Bart had started to protest.

"I mean it, Bart!" The implied threat in Holly's voice was understood.

"I'll 'ave 'em pull out the blinkin' plug," he said. "Though I don't expect our pushin' Pocahontas to ring up Lee. Not now."

So much for the exit of Maxine. The other problem, Holly assured herself, would be somewhat more difficult than the time Dr. Von Engel had switched Lee away from morphine. They had gotten through that night. She would help Lee survive this night, too. And the next and the next, until he was well again.

Even before she had finished telling Lee about the encounter with Maxine, and why she had come back to his suite, Holly realized that she had tackled a job that might be beyond her strength.

"Stay with me through *what?*" he cried from his bed. "Where did she go? Maxine . . . where is she? *Rajah!*" He was frantic. *"Ra-jahh!"* Lee's summons reverberated from the walls. The taciturn male nurse appeared in the doorway leading to his own room, his normally passive face reflecting alarm. "Ring Maxine. Tell her I want her here before —"

"You can't reach her," Holly told him. She decided against angering Lee further by telling him his phone service had been cut off. "Maxine's gone. I saw her leave."

"Where?" Lee demanded. "Where did she go?" When Holly provided no reply he yelled, "Go find her. Don't come back without her, Raj'!"

"He'd better know," Holly lied, "that if he brings her back to this room, she'll be arrested. And so will he."

Rajah had started for the door. Now, torn between two unpleasant choices, he hesitated.

"Lee, don't ask him to jeopardize his freedom," Holly said. "This isn't his problem. It's yours. And mine."

Lee was too distraught to argue. He waved a dismissal, and Rajah crept back to his room, barely able to hide his relief.

"Why did you do it?" Lee asked. It was an agonized question. "Just a few more days. Next Saturday. That was all I wanted. A few more days."

"Your doctor was ready to have you placed in a nursing home," Holly said. "Lee, you need him. Dr. Raymond told me he couldn't keep you as a patient under the circumstances."

"Damned fool doctor! What proof —"

"He knows," Holly said gently. "He knew before I did. Oh, Lee, why didn't you let us help you when —"

"A lot of help you are!" Lee ran a hand over his face, shaky fingers digging into the flesh of his cheek. He sounded close to tears. "This one gig, I thought. Kick it, after that. I wouldn't *need* the stuff once I'd gotten through this one blarsted gig. I've got all the money I'm ever going to need.

We could have gone away. Traveled about. We still can, if . . ." Lee's voice broke. "Why, Holly? *Why?*"

The second "why," screamed at her, brought Holly closer to Lee's bedside. She reached for his hand, but he withdrew it from her reach savagely. "Get out! You heard me. *Get out!* You're dismissed! Tell Raymond he's been sacked, too. You can't be trusted. All this time, plotting against me. Deceitful, rotten, heartless . . ."

"Lee . . ."

For a moment, with Lee's arm raised above his head, Holly thought he might strike out at her. She tensed, ready to avoid the sudden blow. What Lee did was worse. He buried his head in his arms, sobbing like a child.

Holly leaned down to put her arms around him. "Don't, Lee. Please. Please." For a few minutes, stroking his shoulder, then his damp forehead, Holly listened to the racking sobs. It was the beginning of the nightmare against which she thought she had steeled herself, a nightmare that brought Holly face to face with her pitiful ignorance about psychological dependence upon morphine, frightened her with the realization that Glenn Raymond, Bart Mitchell, and, especially, Maxine, had been right; her naive belief that Lee could be nursed through this horror with patience and love was a wishful dream.

Alone with the reality, Holly felt her confidence draining. She could not see herself as a rock to which Lee could cling while he wept, "Don't leave me, Holly. Help me . . . get me through. Please, please, help me get through!" Seconds later, he would be a cursing maniac, vilifying Holly because of his helpless immobility: "If I could crawl out of this bed, I'd break you in two. You're cruel! You're rotten and cruel! You call yourself a nurse. You're a torturer. You know I'm suffering and you've trapped me. Laugh! Go on, laugh! *I-can't-take-any-mo-ore!*"

Then, the pathetic moments of bravado: "Do you think I can't get a fix? I have a million contacts. All I have to do is snap my fingers and I can get anything I want! Harry Terhune, Malay Joe — a word from me and I'll have my stuff." Lee would flail his arm out in a desperate effort to reach the telephone, ignoring Holly's quiet pleas, unreached by the logic of her reasoning. As Lee realized that he was trapped, his fury spent itself on Holly; she was a heartless monster, she was in league with Bart and all of Lee's "so-called friends," they were all plotting to destroy him, and hadn't he suffered enough?

By eleven o'clock, Holly knew that she had made a terrible mistake. Trying to make Lee understand why she had deprived him of the drug was like walking into an insane asylum and explaining to the inmates that it would be ever so much more sensible if they dropped their insanity and started living happy, productive lives. Her do-goodism, her noble intentions, had been built on a false premise, and only an arrogant conceit had led her to believe that she, alone, could offer the golden panacea. Shame and desperation flooded her. Nurse, healer, savior, magician! She was none of these. She was a stupid and stubborn fool, and the blame for Lee's increasing agony could be laid squarely on her conscience.

Still, Holly's nerve did not break, nor did she lose her last tenacious grip on hope, until the physical symptoms that Maxine had predicted began to manifest themselves. She was unqualified to cope with them, too inexperienced to know what the consequences might be if she allowed them to continue. Worse than this was her knowledge that the sudden cramps that ripped Lee's insides would only get worse.

Shivering cold, even under the mound of blankets Holly had supplied, would increase; nausea and maddening hallucinations would render Lee uncontrollable. He might try to escape his bed, hurt himself seriously, perhaps even fatally.

Moments before Lee's soul-stabbing cries for help brought Rajah into the room, Holly's guilt had forced a decision. No humane person could stand by and watch Lee endure the torture of a "cold turkey" withdrawal.

Before Rajah's eyes could accuse her, and before he demanded that help be provided, Holly said, "Rajah, go across the hall to my room . . . the door's unlocked . . . and call Dr. Raymond. The number's on a pad next to my telephone. Don't give up until you've reached him." She hesitated, wondering how to prepare the doctor for what was happening. If he came unprepared . . .

"I understand," Rajah told her. If he resented the responsibility she had taken upon herself, or if he had contempt for her failure and its results, Rajah's impassive features concealed his thoughts. And surely he was no stranger to Lee's addiction. How many times had he watched Maxine prepare the injection? Trained as a male nurse, he had probably plunged the needle into Lee's vein himself. Yet, now, he scurried off obediently, acknowledging Holly's superior authority.

Lee was a tormented wreck by the time Glenn Raymond rushed into the room. The doctor took one look at the patient's perspiration-soaked body, then made a scathing, silent appraisal of Holly's efforts to keep Lee "comfortable." Holly had long before given up illusions of nursing Lee through withdrawal. She was exhausting herself, when the doctor arrived, only in frantic efforts to ease the worst of Lee's symptoms and to keep him from wallowing in filth. More than an hour had elapsed between Rajah's phone call and Glenn Raymond's appearance on the scene. (The doctor had been located, finally, in a hospital emergency room.) During that endless waiting period, there had been several times when all of Rajah's strength, and Holly's, had been needed to restrain Lee from carrying out his screamed intention of crawling to a window and hurling himself into the street below.

Reduced to animal-like moans, pressing his hands against his abdomen, Lee was not aware of anything now except excruciating pain. Certainly he was not conscious of Dr. Raymond's speed in unzipping a black leather bag, or of the doctor's preparation of a hypodermic needle.

More out of habit than in the belief that her assistance would be needed, Holly asked, "What can I do, Dr. Raymond?"

For a seeming eternity he said nothing, concentrating on dropping a tablet into the vial of a sterile syringe, then filling the vial with what Holly guessed was saline solution. Was that a quarter-grain tablet of morphine he was dissolving? Holly wondered. Or was it one of the tranquilizing drugs, like chlorpromazine or reserpine? She didn't dare ask. Her shame before Rajah had been acute, but knowing what Dr. Raymond must be thinking was unbearable.

She thought her question had not only been ignored but forgotten. But as the doctor pulled Lee's left sleeve out of the way, exposing a veritable pincushion of recent needle marks, he murmured, "I should think you have done quite enough, Miss Brooks."

Humiliation burning her cheeks, Holly stood by, her services clearly unwanted, as Dr. Raymond swabbed the area over his patient's deltoid muscle with alcohol. She drew a sharp breath as the needle was plunged into the tense muscle. There was no outcry from Lee; the jab of a hypodermic was a minor pain compared with what he was already enduring.

Holly remained near the bedside, seared by another kind of pain. She had hoped, perhaps presumptuously, for Glenn Raymond's love. Now she had lost even his respect. And the humiliation was intensified because she could not deny his cold criticism. Since Lee's ordeal had started raging beyond control, she had hurled the same insult at herself. The doctor was right; she had done enough. Yet she could not obey the driving instinct to run, to escape, go home and forget this horrible dream.

Mercifully, the injection had quick results. Lee's rigid muscles relaxed, his breathing became less laborious. Holly released an audible sigh of relief when Lee's jaw slackened, his mouth fell open and he slept.

Rajah helped her strip the bed and slip a clean sheet under their patient. Holly worked with an eager, almost manic energy, grateful that she was finally able to be of some value to Lee, but also anxious (though she knew it was a pitiful attempt) to prove that she was a conscientious nurse.

Glenn Raymond stood near the bed throughout this clean-up procedure, his eyes fixed on Lee's face. When there was no doubt that the latter was asleep, he said, more to himself than to the others, "He was too sick and exhausted for the other effect."

It *had* been morphine, then; the doctor was referring to Lee's more typical reaction to the drug, a sudden surge of false energy, a sense of confident, carefree well-being.

Uncomfortable in Dr. Raymond's presence, and too shaken to offer any resistance, Holly only nodded and murmured, "Yes, Doctor," when he said, "Tomorrow I'll arrange to have Mr. Watson moved to Canby." He had mentioned the nursing home-clinic once before; it was a private sanatorium specializing in drug-addiction cases.

Before he left the room, leaving an icy chill behind him, the doctor threw out a barbed *coup de grace*. Holly couldn't have felt more guilt-racked, and the remark struck her as unnecessarily cruel: "At Canby, the professional staff is trained to make withdrawal gradual . . . and humane."

As painful as the words themselves was

the knowledge that they were true, and that they had been spoken by a man Holly had learned to love. It was nearly dawn before Holly sobbed herself into a fitful sleep.

TEN

Guilt plagued Holly again when the ringing telephone awakened her and a glance at her bedside clock, which had been set for seven, told her she had slept through the alarm and it was now nearly ten o'clock.

Shocked out of sleep, she reached for the telephone, positive that the call was a summons from Rajah. Instead, after her querulous greeting, she heard Bart Mitchell's unmistakable voice. "Holly? I was hoping to reach you before you got up. This is Bart, you know."

"Yes, I know. I can't imagine why I overslept. I'll get over to Lee's room as —"

"That's why I called," Bart said evenly. "I didn't want you to get upset."

Holly felt her muscles tense. "What's wrong?" Her mind flashed a series of dire possibilities for which she could be held responsible. "Is Lee —"

"Lee's fine. Fine," Bart said. "He asked me to ring you up so that you wouldn't be worried."

"But I'll be across the hall just as soon as I can get —"

"Holly. . . . Lee isn't there. He's checked out of the hotel."

Holly held her breath through a stunned silence. When she recovered her speech, she asked, "Where is he? How could he have —"

"Rajah called me in after you left him last night. This morning, actually. He told me what was up."

"And you decided to whisk Lee off! Bart, do you know what happened last night? What I did was incredibly stupid, but you've just done something worse. Lee's seriously ill. Dr. Raymond —"

"I know exactly what Raymond intended to do," Bart said. He sounded resigned, even weary, and, as was usual in his more somber moods, there was no trace of his off-and-on accent. "So did Rajah. And so did the Watson when he woke up round about fourish this morning. Ever see a fox hunt? Lee could sniff the hounds at his heels. And no arguing with him. It was either check him out or . . . we'd have had a suicide on our hands. I can't tell you how desperate he was, Holly. If we hadn't cooperated, he'd have felt he didn't have a friend in the world."

159

"But he's got to be under medical care," Holly protested. She was wide awake now, yet what she was hearing seemed like part of an incomprehensible dream.

"He asked me to tell you he'll check into Canby voluntarily, Saturday night. Immediately after the concert. In the meantime, Raj' and the other chap can manage, Lee tells me."

"They can't —"

"They'll *have* to," Bart said. He paused. "I *am* sorry, Holly."

"Are you telling me that Lee doesn't want me around? I can't blame him, after what I put him through, but I —"

"He knew you'd be hurt," Bart said, his tone gentle. "You see, ducks, he's *got* to go through with this concert. You know what it means to him. And it's not that he's angry with you, or that he doesn't trust you —"

"But he doesn't want me to know where he is. He —"

"Because he suspects you'd do the proper thing," Bart cut in. "He *understands*, Holly. He wants you to understand, too. Said he'd ring you up after the rehearsal this afternoon. And all but begged me to convince you that you mustn't leave. Had me arrange a stageside seat for you at the concert. Please, Holly. It's only a matter of hours now. Let me tell him you won't run off and that you aren't angry."

Holly sighed, pressing her eyes shut for a moment. "If anyone has the right to be furious . . ."

"But he's not. He was more concerned about you than anyone else . . . terribly worried about how you'd react to the mass exodus, leaving you at the hotel alone."

"Everyone's gone, then?" Holly assumed the answer. "Tell me something, Bart. How was he feeling? He was so sick last night, I . . ."

"Top-ho. Couldn't be more chipper. Apart from being anxious about you, he was feeling splendid, he said. Had a new song running through his head, and . . . oh, yes, decided to do the vocal on the 'Violet Star' song himself, after all. Couldn't wait to get the group working on it."

"From what you tell me," Holly said bitterly, "he could have had Maxine do the honors. Apparently she's still around. Lee wouldn't be functioning so efficiently if he hadn't gotten his fix this morning."

"We haven't heard from Maxine," Bart said. "Personally, I don't expect we ever will."

"Oh? Then how —"

"Holly, when a man has unlimited means, unlimited imagination, and unlimited numbers of people who'll jump through a fiery hoop at his command, there's always going to be a way for him to get what he wants. There was another groupie bird in the suite when Lee had me rousted out of bed. Don't ask me who she is or how he contacted her. Cut off Hydra's head, a dozen more sprout up. I tried to tell you, you can't stop him. What I'm counting on now is that he's realized how far gone he is and he wants to stop himself. He sounded completely sincere about going in for the cure. Talked about quitting the group, having one smashing success and retiring while he's on top. And marrying you, Holly. I didn't have the time or the heart to discourage him on that point. All I know is, we've got to give him this chance. Believe he's really going to try getting off the stuff. Because of you, he said."

It was useless to debate the subject or to ask where Lee was. Cagily, he wouldn't have gone to his house in Kent or to any other place known to Holly or Dr. Raymond. There was nothing to do but wish him luck and to agree to be present for his "comeback" on Saturday. Beyond that, she could make no promises.

"Have a bit of a holiday," Bart concluded with a forced cheeriness. "See a bit of London. Sorry I can't squire you about. Absolutely rushed with last-minute crises, as you know, but I'll be in touch. And Lee will be, too. Meanwhile, don't struggle along without anything that can be charged to Lee. You have *carte blanche,* so live it up."

"Living it up" in a hotel room in a strange city, with her patient in hiding and his doctor disgusted with her, was an impossible order to fill. Several times during the morning, her conscience aching as painfully as the misery of her unrequited love for Glenn Raymond, Holly thought of phoning the doctor, but each time she was held back by the realization that there was nothing she could say to him, either. His contempt for her wouldn't be erased by a stammering telephone call. What would she say when she reached him?

By the time Holly's fogged mind remembered what she had to say, Glenn Raymond was at her door, more irate than she had ever seen him before.

"I *am* a busy man," he reminded her as Holly ushered him into her room. He hadn't given her a moment in which to apologize. "Common courtesy would have had you let me know that you'd snatched your patient out of my dastardly clutches in the nick of time. I could have seen patients at the clinic this morning instead of conferring with the staff at Canby. I shouldn't have gotten my surprise at the registry desk downstairs."

"I'm sorry," Holly said. The words were beginning to sound hollow, even to her own ears. "I didn't know until —"

"As I told you once before, I'm a doctor, not a police officer. If you wanted to 'protect' Lee Watson from getting proper care, you might have had the decency to let me know. As it is, I canceled my afternoon appointments. Set this time aside for your fiancé." The doctor looked at his watch irritably and turned back toward the door, as if he wondered why he had bothered to come into the room at all. "I expect you're busier than I, packing and what-have-you."

"I'm not packing," Holly told him. "For the simple reason that I'm staying here until after the concert."

"Commuting to your patient's new digs, are you?"

That snide tone again! "I don't know where Lee is!" Holly exploded. "I didn't know he was gone until his manager phoned to tell me! I'm sorry about what I did last night, I'm sorry I let you waste your time today, I'm . . . *I'm sorry I ever left Los Angeles!*" She had given up trying to control her emotions. It didn't matter anymore, and Holly let the tears come. "I don't have any control over Lee Watson. No one does. If you knew him, you wouldn't keep making me the villain of the piece. You're his doctor! Why wasn't he here waiting for you when you came to take him to the nursing home?"

"Because I am merely his doctor," Glenn Raymond said. "I should think the woman he's going to marry would have more —"

"I don't have any influence and I'm not the woman he's going to marry!" Holly cried out. "If you didn't believe everything you read in a sensational gossip sheet, you'd know that."

For a moment, the doctor's expression was one of distrust. Then, his tone almost wistful, he said, "I got the impression from Mr. Watson —"

"Impression, impression! You with your supposed concern with 'the whole patient'! Couldn't you see that I've been a temporary crutch to Lee? Dr. Von Engel saw it. Lee didn't fool him . . . he hasn't even fooled himself. I've been something to cling to until he finds his way again. He'll find that way Saturday and he'll forget I exist."

Holly sank down in one of the armchairs near the window, running a hand over her face. "He hasn't felt anything for me except . . ." Holly hesitated to say "gratitude." It would probably bring a scornful reaction from the doctor. ". . . dependence," she said, finally. "And now he doesn't even trust me enough to let me know where he is."

"It must be painful to . . . to be rejected so abruptly." The doctor spoke hesitantly, as though he still wasn't certain that Holly merited his sympathy. "It's never wise for a nurse to become deeply involved with a patient . . . it's easy to fall in love when —"

"My only emotional involvement has been pity!" Holly said savagely. "Is there something in your code of ethics against feeling compassion for someone who . . ." Holly's sentence dissolved in tears. It was useless to try making this smug, stubborn man understand. "I tried to . . . help Lee," she choked. "I failed. I'd be this miserable if . . . if I'd failed *any* patient. Anyone . . . any human being in the . . . in the world!"

For a while there was no sound in the

room except her own fitful sobbing. Then, in the same moment that Holly felt the gentle touch of hands on her shoulders, Holly heard Glenn Raymond say, "I don't suppose my hypercritical attitude has helped. The apologies should be coming from me, Holly."

She shook her head. "You were right. I tried . . . playing doctor. I knew better."

"I might have been more civilized about that, too, if I hadn't been so childish." The doctor had taken a step forward, so that now he stood at Holly's side. Hands lifted from her shoulder, he tucked one under Holly's chin, raising her tear-stained face upward so that it was impossible to avoid his eyes. "I wasn't very professional, was I? Rabidly envious of a man I have every reason not to envy."

"Envy?" Holly swiped at her cheeks with the back of her wrist. In almost the same instant, her hand was in Dr. Raymond's and he was pressing it tight.

"I wanted to tell you this minutes after I met you. I'd have been jealous of any man you loved, Holly." The doctor made a shy grimace, but his eyes didn't leave Holly's. "That's a rather roundabout way of telling you something that you'll have difficulty believing, girl. I love you."

For a stunned instant, Holly could only stare at him, incredulous, not quite certain that she had heard him correctly. Then, somehow, she had been pulled up to her feet, and incredibly, she was in Glenn Raymond's arms, returning an ardent kiss that conveyed his message more forcefully than his words.

For a long time, Holly clung to him, breathless under the rain of kisses, telling him with the intensity of her embrace that he was loved, too. It seemed redundant, when he finally let her go, for Holly to whisper, "Didn't you know I fell in love with you, too? That first time we met . . . . I was almost sure of it then."

The doctor smiled sheepishly. "And I've been encouraging nothing but the warmest emotions since then."

Holly managed to smile. "Well, I've been wooed more romantically in my day."

"I was a monster."

"You were right most of the time. That was what made me furious." Holly sighed, letting the doctor reassure her with an affectionate hug. "I'll admit I've done some incredibly stupid things. What you didn't know is that Lee Watson's his own man. His manager tried to tell me that. I know now that Lee isn't ever going to do anything he doesn't want to do. All we can do is hope that he wants to kick the drug habit."

Glenn was the serious professional again. "If he's telling himself that he's going to do that because of you, this might not be the best time to tell him about . . ." He made a vague gesture, indicating himself and Holly.

"About us?"

He nodded gravely.

"Tell him I have every intention of marrying you, Holly, and he'll have an excuse not to submit himself to treatment. If, as you say, his love for you is nothing but a crutch, he'll grasp at being 'rejected.' Justify his need for dope."

"Either that, or claim he has no reason to get well," Holly agreed. Her mind was still reeling from the impact of Glenn Raymond's indirect proposal — *"I have every intention of marrying you, Holly"* — but there was no escaping the responsibility that accompanied that joy. "I certainly wouldn't want to tell Lee until he's satisfied himself that he doesn't need me."

"You believe he will?"

"After his concert? Yes. Yes, I'm sure of it. He's going to be a sensation. For one thing, he'll know that his handicap has nothing to do with the reason for his past success. Lee's a fantastic talent. He doesn't have to walk to keep his place at the top."

"We can be patient for a while, can't we?"

Holly returned the squeeze of her hand in the doctor's and his mood brightened. "In the meantime, since we both seem to be unemployed for the rest of the day . . . what would you like to do?"

"I don't know, Doctor."

The incongruity of using formal terms when they had been exchanging fervent kisses a moment before struck them both as funny.

"I think you can safely call me by my Christian name," Glenn said with mock seriousness.

"What would *you* like to do, Glenn?"

They talked about driving out to see the Kew Gardens, then wondered whether it might not be fun, in spite of the overcast skies, to get Moulton bicycles from what Glenn called a "hire shop" and ride around one of the numerous parks that dotted the city. They had embellished the latter idea with a picnic, and, possibly, seeing a play that evening, when Holly remembered the expected telephone call from Lee. "He'd be terribly upset if he couldn't reach me," she said. "He'd assume I'd gotten angry and headed for the airport. And then he'd be all racked up with guilt."

"*Or* fury, *or* self-pity," Glenn predicted. "Another excuse, and he's so hooked physiologically that he doesn't need any excuses. Still, you can't stay cooped up in this room waiting for him to ring you up. From what I've seen of Watson, he's liable to get involved with his music and —"

"— forget I exist," Holly concluded. "I hope he does, Glenn, for his sake. Just the same, I . . . would you be terribly annoyed if I told you my conscience won't bother me as much if I wait for the call?"

Glenn understood. It didn't really matter that the day was spent within paging distance of the hotel's switchboard; their newly discovered love for each other, the dreamlike fact that they would spend the rest of their lives together, would have carried them through far duller circumstances. It was enough to be with each other.

It wasn't an ironic blow to Holly that the call, for which she and Glenn Raymond had sacrificed a day of enjoying the sights of London, didn't come until well past eleven that night, when she was alone.

Somehow, it wasn't even important that Lee's voice was drowned out by the pounding of drums and the twang of an electric guitar, so that Holly understood nothing of what he had to say, and was certain that Lee couldn't have heard her words, either. What *did* matter was that Lee was still functioning. After Saturday, hopefully, he would not need Holly or the drug she had denied him.

Eleven

Although the free concert was not scheduled to begin until three o'clock Saturday afternoon, young people had started converging on the park twenty-four hours earlier. Glenn and Holly saw the early arrivals on television Friday night, the grounds illuminated by flickering (and illegal) campfires, thousands of the faithful lugging sleeping bags and blankets to ward off the damp chill of night, devotedly and doggedly holding their place near the mammoth bandstand.

By ten on Saturday morning, all access roads to the park were hopelessly snarled in traffic, and public transportation had become a chaos of jammed-together bodies, stalled buses, and exasperated bobbies. In spite of the confusion, a record-breaking crowd was on hand to hear the two lesser groups that were to precede the appearance of Lee Watson and the Tree of Life.

"It's incredible," Glenn Raymond kept repeating. Standing in the wings of the bandshell, recovering from the hectic limousine trip Bart Mitchell had arranged, the doctor and Holly could only see half of the assembled throng, yet it seemed to them that every human being under thirty had managed to be present for Lee's first performance since his accident.

It *was* an incredible sight, a staggering sea of humanity, and in spite of the crowding and the heat from an untypically strong sun, there had been no unpleasant incidents. Several people had fainted, and it was reported that one of the ambulances had roared away carrying an imminent mother-to-be, but a holiday atmosphere pervaded. That, and an almost worshipful air of expectancy; Lee had come home. Placards held up by excited teeny-boppers welcomed him. One of the largest home-made signs, held aloft by a pretty trio of girls, seemed to express the sentiments of everyone present. Simply, and poignantly, it recognized the tragedy of their idol. It read, *WE LOVE YOU MORE THAN EVER, LEE.*

Bart had provided folding chairs for the special guests who were permitted to occupy this stageside area, but no one used them. Somehow, the contagious excitement (and for those who knew what this afternoon meant to Lee) the tension made it impossible to sit down and relax.

Surrounded by Lee's business associates and favored members of the press, Holly found it almost impossible to carry on a conversation with Glenn. Once, when the doctor asked if she thought they could get back to the dressing rooms to see Lee, reminding Holly that Lee had not had the benefits of any medical care since his abrupt departure from the hotel, her reply was drowned out by polite applause for the arrival on stage of a fill-in group called the Catalyst. It was polite applause, rendered thunderous only by the sheer magnitude of the crowd; these thousands had assembled to hear Lee Watson, and anyone else who appeared was merely helping to pass the time until that great moment.

Two interruptions helped to fill that time for Holly. One came about when Bart Mitchell, looking more harried than usual, rushed by on his way to check something with the Tree of Life's equipment manager. "Can't talk to you now, ducks," he panted as Holly waved at him.

"I just wondered if we couldn't see Lee for a moment. Can we get back to the dressing rooms?" It wasn't necessary to keep her voice down; the insistent beat from the stage would have overcome a loud yell.

"He'll see you after the show," Bart called back. "He's ironing out a few last-minute changes. After . . ." Bart was swept away by two sound engineers who intercepted his contact with the young man responsible for the group's instruments and amplifiers. Everything Bart had to do had to be done at the same time. Presumably his star was in condition to perform without the aid of a doctor or a nurse.

The second interruption was made by a uniformed messenger, who fought his way through the milling crowd of privileged people in the wings with the aid of a grim-faced bobby. He carried a monstrous bouquet of deep-red roses, which, after he had asked Holly to identify herself, he presented to her before disappearing into the backstage bedlam.

"Here . . . you'll collapse under the weight," Glenn said. He relieved Holly of the enormous bouquet, which hid her face and was impossibly awkward to hold. As Holly searched the mass of roses for a clue to their sender, the doctor asked, "Who sent them, darling? Someone interested in setting you up with a florist's shop?"

Holly knew before she located the gift card who had sent the roses; it was the sort of flamboyant and impractical gesture that might occur to Lee. Her guess was correct. Apparently written by someone in the flower shop, for the handwriting was not Lee's, the card read, *"Sorry, little bride. Life should be all roses for you with a new violet star in the heavens. Luv, L."*

Holly read the bewildering message twice before handing it to Glenn, saying, "It's from Lee."

Glenn had set the unmanageable mass of roses on one of their reserved chairs. Did his frown result from the intimacy of Lee's note, or was he only puzzled by its obscure meaning? Evidently both factors bothered him. "He seems to be assuming a marriage, Holly. I don't make much sense out of it, but I know that a man doesn't . . . I shouldn't think he'd refer to you as his 'little bride' without *some* encouragement."

Holly made an exasperated face. "I can't dictate what other people write to me," she said. "I've told you the truth, Glenn. You can make whatever you want out of it."

Glenn apologized hastily. "I believe you. I didn't mean to imply . . ."

For a few seconds, the Catalyst's thumping rhythm made it impossible to hear anything else. Then, anxious to avoid another misunderstanding with Glenn,

Holly explained, "I suppose Lee meant that everything's going to be fine because he's going to Canby after this concert." That explained the bit about everything being "roses." "One of his new songs is called 'Violet Star.' Trust Lee to be poetic. And obscure."

"Off on a drug cloud," Glenn said tersely. He returned the card to Holly, and no more was said about Lee Watson's intended message. By the time the Catalyst had played its set, going off without any demands for encores, and the second group (an American import with a title that sounded like, but probably wasn't, the Inevitable Albatross) was in full swing, the deep-red roses drooped on their stems, their petals wilting.

A restlessness seized the audience when the American group launched an unexpected fourth number. Although their music sounded infectious, even exciting, to Holly, a mumbling discontent could be heard from the throng facing the bandstand.

"They're going to start a row if Watson doesn't come on soon," Glenn predicted.

Holly nodded. At the same time her attention was arrested by activity in the wings on the other side of the stage. It was difficult to see through the maze of instruments and gyrating performers, but she caught a glimpse of Desmond, black and majestic in what appeared to be a purple velvet blouse trimmed with gold braid. By straining her vision, she made out other members of the Tree of Life; the drummer's curly yellow Harpo Marxish hair, bass guitarist Mark Ainsley's carrot-colored mop and beard. She was beginning to feel uneasy, worried that Lee had not been up to making an appearance, when she caught sight of Lee's wheelchair. Actually, only the shining chrome spokes of one wheel were visible through the human obstacles between herself and Lee, but Holly felt a sense of relief. What had made her think there was something wrong?

A surge of excitement gripped the audience as the second group bowed off, and the Tree of Life's equipment crew went to work. By the time the sound engineers and set-up men left the stage, the crowd was in a wild state of anticipation. Minutes later, the master of ceremonies had gotten as far as, "And now, the moment we have all been waiting for," when an ear-splitting ovation exploded from Lee's fans. Holly barely heard the shouted introduction *"Lee Watson and the Tree of Life!"*

It seemed that the screaming, clapping, cheering sound couldn't possibly rise to a higher level. Yet, as Lee wheeled himself onstage, followed by the other members of his group, the volume of that thunderous reception rose to a deafening pitch, and there was no indication that it would ever subside.

Lee turned his chair to face his audience, waving cheerfully, a wide, pleased smile radiating from his handsome face. How could you define the electricity of his presence? Holly wondered. "Charisma" was too weak a word to describe Lee's unique magnetism. He had not lost that indefinable ingredient that drew people to him and made him the master of any scene. But another ingredient had been added; Lee could not escape knowing that part of this display of affection for him was based on sympathy.

As the emotional reception continued — if anything, rising in volume — Holly found tears dimming her view of the brightly attired figure in the center of the stage. She glanced around her to see that others were similarly affected. There were few dry eyes among the people who had gathered in the wings. A portly man who was part of the Tree of Life's publicity team stared out at the stage, huge tears rolling down his face. A young woman who covered the music scene for a French newspaper held a handkerchief to her mouth, her shoulders shaking, weeping openly.

Bart materialized again during the long ovation. He was not untouched, but enthusiasm rode over his more poignant emotion. "Beautiful!" Holly heard him say. "Try telling Lee *now* that 'e's finished!"

Lee, appearing far from "finished," made several attempts to wave down the tumult. At least fifteen minutes elapsed before the fans responded to his attempt to quiet them. Even then, the silence was not complete until Desmond placed the guitar in Lee's lap and Harvey Scott began a driving drum beat to launch the group's first number. It was a thumping rock piece Lee had written to include the sounds of a jet landing and to simulate the insane excitement of his arrival at the airport. It was a purely instrumental effort called "Heathrow Homecoming," and it was received with the same tumultuous approval that had greeted Lee's appearance.

Bart, applauding as though he hadn't heard the song in countless rehearsals kept saying, "Beautiful . . . beautiful!" to no one in particular. He repeated the phrase after a full set of "new sound" songs, during which Lee demonstrated conclusively that he was still at the top of the heap as an inventive composer, arranger, musician, and singer.

It was during the fifth song that it happened; a shocking indifference on Lee's part that seemed to bewilder the other musicians as much as the audience.

"What's 'e *doing?*" Holly heard Bart ask.

Lee's back-up instrumentalists, who had picked up his earlier inspired performances like reflecting mirrors, responded, at first, with a studied effort to pick up the lagging tempo. Harvey Scott, especially, beat out exaggerated accents, as though trying to reacquaint Lee with the rhythm. It was hopeless. Lee not only floundered rhythmically, he treated the melodic line as though it didn't exist, and at several points, he mumbled his own lyrics in a monotone that made them incomprehensible.

"He's had a lapse of memory," someone in the wings whispered fearfully.

Bart shook his head back and forth, as though he didn't believe anything of the kind. Like everyone else, his eyes remained fixed on the star, his expression grim.

"It's the drug wearing off," Glenn confided to Holly.

She pressed her fingernail against her palms, dreading a possible collapse. Or, worse, an emotional breakdown; Lee wheeling himself off the stage, convinced that his career was ended.

Lee's song came to no specific conclusion; his voice drifted off as though he had suddenly tired of singing, leaving a void of embarrassed silence. Unaccountably, or perhaps because his loyal supporters felt that Lee's ability could be resurrected by appreciation, the fiasco was followed, after that moment of uneasy quiet, by a tremendous round of applause.

Strange, too, was Lee's reaction. Instead of appearing depressed by what he must have known was an abominable performance, he looked out at his audience with a cooly confident expression. And, although he acknowledged the applause with a smile, it was a bitter, knowing smile, almost as though he had put his listeners to a test and they had behaved predictably.

Holly's dread melted during the next song, the experimental "country-baroque" combination in which Lee was joined vocally by Desmond (who was also featured in an organ solo) and the player, Norb Sutliffe. It was a fantastic new departure in music, and when Lee yodeled a punning lyric, "Carry me Bach to the lone pray-ree-ee," embellishing it with hilarious gestures, the crowd screamed its delight.

"Incredible" had replaced "Beautiful" in Bart Mitchell's vocabulary. He was as amazed as everyone else by the sharpness of Lee's rendition; the debacle of the previous song seemed like a forgotten bad dream.

Yet that stunning blow was to be repeated not once, but three times more during the next half hour. The tension that made Bart's veins stand out like taut wires on his temples permeated the atmosphere. And Holly found herself gripping Glenn Raymond's hand in an attempt to steady herself as Lee garbled his way through songs that she had heard him perform flawlessly during rehearsals.

During the fourth of the incomprehensible lapses, during which the nervousness of Lee's fellow musicians transferred itself to everyone present, Holly began to understand why Bart had shaken his head at the suggestion that Lee was suffering a lapse of memory.

To begin with, Lee not only knew his

material, he knew it so well that he was able to take liberties with it. What was missing, she realized, was the inimitable quality called "soul" that distinguished the performance of a second-rate talent from that of an artist. From experience in listening to Lee when he poured his heart into his music, Holly concluded that his sloppy rendition was deliberately so; he was withholding an emotional commitment, refusing to give of himself, almost arrogantly letting his audience know that they could not have all of him. Not all of the time. When he chose to share the essence of Lee Watson, yes. But there were no guarantees; there were times when he belonged only to himself. There was no more doubt, in anyone who knew him, that Lee's erratic performance was a perverse game. If his plan was to demonstrate that the Tree of Life was just another of thousands of rock groups without him, he was succeeding admirably. But Lee seemed to have another motive. It came to Holly when the hackneyed, bumbling rendition ended and the audience cheered Lee's inspired renditions.

"They don't seem to know the difference, do they?" Holly said to Bart.

Bart sniffed, not even bothering to pre

tend that he was not close to tears. "They know, duckie," he said in a solemn tone. "They know the difference, all right." He looked inexpressibly sad. "I just wish they weren't taking the bait. Lord, if only they'd boo and hiss! Let him *know* he can't get away with it."

"You think he's doing it deliberately, then." Holly didn't pose a question; she knew the answer as well as Bart. Lee was determining how far he could go, insulting his audience, probing to find out what part pity and nostalgia played in their admiration for him. It was horrible to contemplate, but he had gotten his answer; Lee's fans would have applauded him if he had sung "God Save the Queen" off key. Because he had come before them in a wheelchair. Because he was hopelessly crippled. *Because they pitied him?*

Holly's fingers curled more tightly around Glenn's. She heard him say, "There ought to be something we can do for him, Holly. Get him through this . . ." And then Glenn's words died out, along with the applause, as a cymbal crashed and Desmond brought a plaintive, minor-keyed theme from the organ. Did the audience know that this was to be the last song Lee would sing for them this evening, and that he would invest it with all of the magic, all of the mystery that made up his psyche?

A respectful hush fell over the entire park area. It was an eerie atmosphere, as though thousands of people had suddenly been overcome by the same awesome sensation. To Holly, the aura was as touching, as suspenseful, as the moments she remembered in the hospital, when a patient hovered between life and death.

Desmond had established an otherworldly mood, and Harvey's slow, hollow drum beat had established an ominous feeling that contrasted with the gentle chords that followed, muted as if heard through an echo chamber, from Lee's guitar. Holly saw him close his eyes, his expression one of childish, almost saintly innocence.

At the beginning, Holly was so moved by the crystal purity of Lee's voice and the tenderness with which he sang that she was barely aware of the lyric. She remembered Lee saying that the song called for a soft, ephemeral, feminine voice, yet it was impossible, now, to imagine anyone else singing it. Holly had listened to the song being discussed, but she had not heard it before. Listening closely, duplicating the rapt attention of everyone around her, she strained to understand the words that drifted along the hauntingly beautiful melody:

> *"I could have loved you, if I had*
> *known how,*
> *If love is a dream, then I need to*
> *dream now,*
> *And I'll tell you I've learned or I've*
> *failed, from afar*
> *Through all time, through the mists*
> *from a violet star."*

Lee's words had a disturbingly personal ring to them, but perhaps this was the effect Lee had strived for; every girl listening was probably convinced that he was singing only to her. Still, Lee had declared his love for Holly. Was he admitting that he was incapable of love — at least, the selfless, undivided love that he knew would be expected of him? And when his untypically simple lyric spoke of a faraway place, from which he could only communicate "through the mist," was he speaking of his imprisonment in a drugged world, virtually another dimension, as unreachable to others as a distant star?

Whatever the words were intended to mean, "Violet Star" was a love song, or, more precisely, a farewell to love. Nor was there any further question about whether or not Lee was in control of himself. Holly had never heard him express himself musically with more delicate precision, so that even his superbly timed pauses evoked deep emotions. Never before had his communication with others been more complete. When he repeated the last line of the chorus, the words were almost whispered: *"Through all time, through the mists . . . from a violet star,"* the breathless silence was broken by a choked sob from somewhere out in the audience. Unconsciously, Holly's glance searched for a tiny dark-haired girl in a fringed-leather squaw costume, but the cry could have come from anyone touched by the spiritual quality of Lee's voice.

His guitar sobbed an echo to that sound from beyond the bandstand, and Lee lowered his head. This time the quiet that followed was not caused by embarrassment. It was more like an audience hesitating to applaud a sermon or a hymn, anxious to express its approval, yet wondering if applause might be improper, even sacrilegious.

As Lee raised his head, then swung hi guitar to the floor and turned his whe chair toward the wings, the crowd's hesitancy broke. Lee was wheeling himself offstage rapidly, leaving the rest of his group to watch him in bewilderment, the applause more enthusiastic than that which had greeted his first appearance.

"Where's 'e going?" Bart yelled. "They haven't played 'alf . . ." Apparently Bart decided to take charge of the situation. Holly saw him dart onstage, hold a hurried conversation with Desmond, and then hurry after Lee, who had, by then, gone beyond Holly's view or that of the audience.

At the first indication that the applause was dying down, the remaining four members of the Tree of Life burst into a hit song from their old repertoire, a number that featured a drum solo by Harvey Scott and a chant in unison by the entire group. Familiar with the music, the crowd seemed assured that Lee would return in time for the vocal, probably assuming that his departure was planned and only temporary.

A disquieting instinct told Holly that this was not so. "Is there a way to get to the other side without crossing the stage?" she asked Glenn. She had to shout against his ear to be heard over the drums. "I'm worried about Lee."

"I was about to suggest that we swing around the back, here, and see." Glenn indicated the rear of the bandstand, taking Holly's arm at the same time and guiding her through the groups of people who had gathered behind them. "I'm sure that Mitchell chap came through here earlier," he said.

They found a narrow, semicircular passageway that followed the contours of the shell. Three unshaded light bulbs illuminated the curved tunnel. It was deserted, and, somehow, uninviting, allowing space for only one person to pass through at a time. Glenn led the way.

As they passed the area paralleling the back center of the stage, where Harvey Scott's drums were set up, it was like being caught in the middle of a battlefield.

Maybe it was only the deafening volume of the drums at this close range, but Holly felt a sudden pang of fear, as though the nerves that held her together had been stretched beyond their tensile strength and threatened her with collapse. She hesitated, and Glenn turned around, probably guessing Holly's tension from a glance at her face. Nothing he could have said to her would have been heard over Harvey Scott's rhythmic *tour de force*. Instead, Glenn took

Holly's hand, gave it a reassuring squeeze, and led her forward.

They had barely emerged into the wide area on the other side of the stage when Glenn made a sudden stop. In almost the same instant, Holly saw Bart Mitchell racing toward the backstage passageway, a look of indescribable horror distorting his features.

Bart had evidently been rushing to get the doctor. Gasping for breath, his voice trembling, he cried, "Come — quick! Lee's shot himself! It's probably too late. I — oh, my God, I think he's dead!"

TWELVE

Bart must have known, when he ran out of Lee's dressing room to summon the doctor, that nothing more could be done for his friend. Yet he had clung desperately to a slender hope, because the alternative was too unbearable to accept. It wasn't until Glenn had raised his head from the bloody form slouched in the wheelchair, his lips forming a nearly soundless "I'm sorry. He's gone," not until then did Bart turn to Holly, too numbed by the shock to cry, too grief stricken to do anything else, reaching his arms out to hold her, but also to be held.

For a while, the little manager and Holly clung to each other, still unable to perceive their loss. Beyond the star's dressing room, Harvey was exhausting himself in a frenzied extension of his solo, thrilling the audience with a virtuoso performance while he and his fellow musicians waited for a leader who would never return. If Lee had planned his suicide meticulously (and he must have; not even Bart or Rajah knew where he had obtained the revolver tha had been discharged into his heart) he could not have anticipated the thunder-storm of percussion that had made the gunshot inaudible.

Bart did not indulge his grief too long. There was still a service he could perform for his boyhood chum. "We can't let word get out there," he choked, his head gesturing in the general direction of the audience.

Holly remembered Lee's homecoming at the airport and shuddered. There would be no controlling the more hysterical and morbid of Lee's fans if the ghastly news spread through that crowd.

Helping Bart eased the shock. There were calls to make, instructions to give to the M.C., and the Tree of Life. Keep playing. Stall for time until Lee's body can he secretly removed. Above all else, don't risk the riot that would inevitably result if the largest audience ever assembled to hear a performer learned that their idol had killed himself.

It was managed. So, too, was the private funeral three days later, word of its time and location as tightly guarded as any crucial military secret. Holly was not alone in weeping like a child as Desmond, at the keyboard of the chapel organ, played the last strains of the farewell song Lee had written for himself. Outside the chapel, a swirling fog simulated the mists that separated Lee's home on a "violet star" from the company of mourners. It seemed to Holly that the sun hadn't shined in years. The mists thickened into a depressing drizzle before Lee's casket was lowered into the ground.

Bart and the musicians who had been part of Lee Watson's life were inconsolable. Holly clung to Glenn's arm as they walked back to the limousine across a soggy turf. Only Maxine remained to watch the gravesite covered with floral pieces; a forlorn and silent figure in wet buckskin, tearless, letting the skies weep for her while she kept her lonely vigil.

Glenn had the good sense to know that nothing he could say or do would change Holly's sense of unreality. He saw her directly to her hotel and returned to his patients. Tears would wash away the numbed sensation, and time would heal the scar of having grown close to a complex, gifted young man whose life, rich with potential, had been senselessly cut short. But what would erase the pain of wondering if she, and an old physician she had always deeply respected, had contributed to Lee Watson's death? Lee must have felt himself hopelessly trapped in the nightmare of his addiction. How could a doctor who had been too late in cutting a patient off from morphine escape responsibility? More personally, how could a nurse who had spent most of Lee's waking hours at his side declare herself blameless? Holly wept as bitterly over what had happened as for what might have been if she had not, somehow, failed her patient.

Emotionally drained, she was unprepared for the aftershock that came to her late the next afternoon by way of two telephone calls. Glenn had phoned earlier to suggest that they have dinner together that evening, to "discuss future plans." When the telephone rang at four-twenty, Holly guessed that Glenn might be calling back to change their plans; he carried a heavy patient load which made canceling dates the norm rather than the exception for him.

Instead of hearing Glenn's voice when she answered, Holly was greeted by Bart Mitchell's unmistakable voice. "Hullo, ducks. I've been worried about you."

"Worried?"

"Well, you know . . . stranded in a strange place, and all that. Fortunately,

I've been busy, looking after Lee's affairs. Morbid details, but at least I've 'ad no time to brood. The group's completely demoralized. Can't seem to do anything but smoke cigarettes and pace floors. I've 'ad you on my conscience . . . all alone and nothing to occupy your mind."

Holly assured Bart that she hadn't expected him to drop his work to look after her. For a few minutes, they talked in subdued tones about Lee's death, its impact on those who had been close to him, and the fact that newspapers were still covering every aspect of the story.

"The commercial ghouls are working frantically," Bart lamented. "Trying to be first on the market with books and magazines and fake mementos. It sickens me, really. You're going to be disgusted with all the vultures who come crowding round you when this other news breaks. I was hoping it wouldn't leak out until you'd gotten yourself settled, whatever you plan to do. You're going to be awfully vulnerable in a London hotel, I'm afraid. One of my reasons for ringing you up was to suggest that you move out to . . ."

Holly gave up trying to understand what was being said to her. "Bart? What *are* you talking about?"

"Lee's will. His attorneys were going to contact you tomorrow morning, but apparently the word filtered out prematurely. He left everything to you, Holly. Except for token sums to his staff, you're the sole beneficiary."

It was still incomprehensible. "I don't understand. Bart, that can't be true! He knew me only a short time. There were so many people who were closer to him." Holly had been standing. Now she sank to the edge of her bed. "There's got to be some mistake."

Bart's voice seemed to be coming from another planet. "No mistake," he was saying. "I've known about it since Lee made the change in his will. All of it, old girl. I ought to tell you that what with investments and future royalties on albums, it should amount to well over a million pounds, before taxes."

"But the group . . . the Tree of Life . . ."

"They won't have to be concerned about rent money ever in their lives," Bart said. "No one who was associated with Lee can be called impoverished. He used to say that a musician had only two incentives — to make music and, or, to make money. And once he told me that he didn't want to take either incentive away from the chaps who came up with him."

Holly was only half listening now, her thoughts flashing back to the message Lee had sent with a bouquet of roses that, in the aftermath of his death, had been left on a chair inside a park band-shell. "Life should be all roses for you with a new violet star in the heavens." That had been Lee's way of telling Holly that his demise would make her wealthy! Why hadn't she caught the warning, rushed after him when he deserted the stage after what was so obviously recognizable now as a suicide ballad?

She was too shaken to hear all of Bart's practical suggestions, only mumbling a vague assent to his advice that she move out of the hotel before the news hounds cornered her. Or, worse, before rivals for Lee's money converged upon the scene.

"I'll send someone around immediately to help you get moved," Bart promised. "Stay in touch, duckie. I can't help thinking of you as my little sister."

Holly dropped the receiver convinced that Bart was right; she wasn't up to interviews or arguments, and the thought of being hounded by morbid curiosity seekers terrified her. She could save time, before Bart sent someone to help expedite her ove, if she started packing. First, though, she should contact Glenn, arrange to meet him elsewhere.

As usual, Glenn was not easily reached. Holly's luggage had been carried down to a waiting limousine in the hotel garage, and she was ready to abandon her room, to resume her attempt to reach Glenn from whatever hideaway Bart had arranged for her, when the telephone shrilled.

It was Glenn. And in one sentence, "I understand you've been trying to contact me," the doctor's chill formality told Holly that something was wrong.

She was in the midst of explaining why she was making a sudden move when Glenn interrupted, "I've just heard the news from one of my patients. She'd heard it on the telly a few minutes earlier. I expected you might want to go into hiding." There was a stiff pause, after which Holly hoped he would name a different place for their meeting. Instead, he said crisply, "I suppose congratulations are in order."

"Glenn . . . you sound as though —"

"I sound exactly the way you should expect me to. I can't possibly feel otherwise about people who want to have their cake and eat it, too."

"I don't even know what that's supposed

to mean!" Holly protested.

"When you were so quick to agree that poor Watson shouldn't be told about our relationship, I was stupid enough to attribute your agreement to compassion."

"But what other reason —"

"You weren't about to jeopardize your position with a drug-addicted cripple who couldn't have gone on living for terribly long in any event. Not when you'd managed to get him to announce his intention of marrying you."

"I didn't 'manage' anything of the kind!" Holly argued, her anger rising. "I told you those gossip columnists —"

"The columnists were only quoting what they'd heard from Watson. In your presence and mine, incidentally."

"I explained that to you, Glenn. You understood why I —"

"I *mis*understood," he cut in. "I should have taken my exit clue from that note Watson sent to you before his concert. 'Little bride.' He knew he was going to end his life, but you'd given him no reason to suppose that you weren't going to be his wife."

"But I wasn't . . . I didn't even *love* him, except as —"

"My point," Glenn said. "My point exactly. I'm sorry, Holly. I had marvelously high hopes for us. You can't know how disappointed, how completely disillusioned I am."

Her mind reeled. Was Glenn telling her that he thought she had led a doomed man to believe she loved him because she wanted to inherit his money? It was too monstrous, too cruel; Glenn couldn't think so little of her! Yet, before Holly could recover enough to express her shock, she heard Glenn saying, "Please don't let me delude myself again. I'd very much appreciate a civilized goodbye and . . . getting back to my work."

She was breathing hard, still unable to believe that Glenn's accusation had been made seriously. "It's not true," she cried. "Nothing you're saying . . . none of it is true!" Her voice had climbed to a strident pitch, and apparently an emotional scene, even one that was justified, was not in keeping with Glenn's idea of a "civilized goodbye." Holly was crying, arguing, berating him for having lowered her to the most scurrilous level, telling him that the will, of which she'd had no knowledge, would inevitably be contested and that she would make no attempt to fight the challengers, when the soft but unmistakable click of a receiver cut her off. The humming sound of an open line taunted her, more devastating than the sound of a door that had been slammed forever.

She would have time for regret later, time enough for the agony of heartbreak. Now it was pure blinding rage that propelled her out of the room. The telephone was shrilling as she closed the door behind her. If the news had already been broadcast, newspapermen were probably at the registry desk by now. Holly ignored the ringing phone and made her way through the labyrinth of back corridors that led to the underground garage.

Lee's ex-chauffeur, who had helped whisk her luggage downstairs, leaped out from the driver's seat to open a back door of the limousine. He must have noticed her agitated expression, because, as the Rolls Royce eased up the ramp into the street, he offered a comforting assurance: "You won't be harassed at the house in Belgravia, miss. It's quite secluded and Mr. Watson always kept its ownership quite secret."

"I won't be going there," Holly told him. She chewed on her lower lip for a moment, hesitating before a decision that would end forever her chances of a reconciliation with

Glenn. Then she said, "Drive me to Heathrow, please."

"To the airport, miss?" The chauffeur's astonishment was reflected back from the rear view mirror. "Mr. Mitchell gave me instructions —"

"I've changed my plans," Holly told him. "I'm going back to the United States."

The driver was silent for a few moments while he wrangled his way into a traffic lane. Then, apparently caught between conflicting but equally adamant orders, he ventured, "Do you have a reservation, Miss Brooks? We could stop at Mr. Mitchell's office and arrange for your flight. Otherwise, you might have a tiring wait . . ."

"I have my reservation," Holly lied. To have admitted otherwise would have meant long explanations and the ordeal of having Bart talk her into staying. A long wait at the airport would be less painful than the longer, perhaps endless, wait for Glenn Raymond's apology.

Her words must not have sounded too convincing. "If you say so, miss," the chauffeur said. Discreetly, he said nothing more during the rest of their drive to the air terminal, and if he was aware of Holly's tears, he did not find them unusual; a great many young women had been seen crying during the past four days in London. Certainly it was expected that Lee Watson's fiancé, the heiress to his fortune, would shed more tears than his fans.

Thirteen

Holly had been alternating for several hours between a padded bench in one of the waiting lounges and the desk of an overseas airline when she returned, once more, to her seat. Her ticket was finally tucked into her handbag, her luggage checked. Another two-hour wait yawned before her, and she was beginning to have qualms about leaving without the simple courtesy of a phone call to Bart Mitchell when she saw him scurrying across the vast terminal toward her more secluded airline lounge. He had evidently seen her, for he was making a hasty beeline in her direction.

Seconds later, embarrassed and almost too wrung out for explanations, Holly found Bart sitting beside her, assailing her with a rapid-fire monologue.

"You're as bad as Lee, thinking you can run away from yourself! If Charles wasn't as perceptive as he is, you'd have flown off without so much as a fare-thee-well. It's not cricket, you know. I thought we were good friends, duckie. Good friends don't *do* what you're doing."

There was nothing to do but apolog.
and tell him why she was running. Ba.
waved her silent before she had finished
telling him about the depressing conversation with Glenn.

"I know all about that," he said irritably.
"You can't blame the man, really. When a
chap's in love with a bird, he can't help
being sensitive. Of course, he can ring you
back seconds later to tell you he's sorry
and find you don't answer. The doc
phoned me directly afterward, but all I
could tell him was that you were probably
on your way to the townhouse in Belgravia.
Poor chap had to dash over there before he
rang me up again. By that time the chauffeur had reported to me that you were
here." Bart looked out across the terminal,
as though looking for someone. "I expect
he's somewhere about, doing a frantic
search for you."

"Why?" Holly asked. "Why would he
want to go searching for me, when he's already pegged me as a mercenary liar?"

"Because he's a man and he's in love
with you and he probably can't imagine a
millionairess settling down to being the
wife of a British doctor. Our medics don't
earn what yours do, y'know." Bart said it

ost accusingly. "In addition to which, it rather difficult for anyone who didn't now Lee to understand why he left the whole bundle to you."

Holly made a disparaging remark about the kind of love that is influenced by mere money. Bart was too annoyed to listen to her. "I told Doc Raymond and I may as well tell you. It's like speaking evil of the dead, and I'd rather 'ave not. Holly — get it through your lovely little 'ead. He was a study in contradictions. Lee could be as kind and as generous as a saint, and then as petty and vindictive as you can imagine. You had to love his genius to be able to love him, because nothing else counted in his life. The will . . . you think he wasn't thinking of the turmoil that would cause when he wrote it? And, incidentally, it was made while he was recovering in Los Angeles. At a time when he had to ask someone what your last name was!"

"I'm . . . getting tired of saying that I don't understand," Holly said.

"But you don't. All right. Lee was married twice. I managed to keep it quiet, both marriages, both divorces. Nice birds. Madly in love with him. But they couldn't *live* with him. It was pure hell for those girls. One had the sense to get out while she had her sanity. The other, Lee dumped as though she were so much rubbish. He used people, Holly. I don't think he wanted to — it was his nature. When I argued with him about that insane will, he told me it would be 'kicky' to know that his ex-wives would have to scramble in court to get a share. Sheila, by the way, 'as never asked for five bob, and if Lee 'ad ever known I juggled his books to send her a monthly check, he'd have thrown me out. The girl married him when he was scrounging about for a gig in Soho dives, and she 'as a son. Kept hoping Lee would come around to see the boy someday. Fall in love with 'er again, if she didn't annoy him."

Holly listened in stunned silence. This was Lee's best friend speaking; a man whose devotion to the star could never be questioned.

"Do you wonder I was relieved when you told me you weren't in love with our boy?" Bart's eyes had gotten moist, and he paused to compose himself. "I'd 'ave laid down an' died for Lee," he said after a while. "But I couldn't ever call him an admirable character. He was a victim of . . ." Bart shrugged. ". . . whatever it was that drove him."

Holly listened closely, yet it was hard to

keep her eyes from straying, looking across the terminal in search of an excitingly familiar figure. (Bart had said that Glenn was *here*. He had tried to call her back to apologize. He had, in Bart's words, been "frantic"!)

"I tried to tell you how futile it was . . . trying to buck the drug thing," Bart went on. "All Lee had to know was that someone didn't want 'im to do what 'e was doing. That was always an irresistible challenge to him."

Holly shook her head. "The drug situation was different. It wasn't Lee's fault that he got hooked. It wasn't just stubbornness, Bart. Complete physiological dependence. The body begins to demand morphine. It's like air or water; Lee *couldn't* exist without it. The suffering . . ." She shuddered, recalling her misguided attempt to break Lee of the habit. "Don't think I don't have that on my conscience. I won't ever free myself of it. Dr. Von Engel was berating himself before we left Los Angeles."

Bart was looking at her with wide-eyed concern. "You can't blame yourself for that. Holly . . . that's insane! Lee was a drug freak when he was fourteen. Not the heavy stuff, true, but he'd run the whole gamut long before you ever laid eyes on him."

"He wasn't addicted to morphine," Holly argued. "That happened in the hospital."

"It was the next step. 'Fact, he *told* me it would be. He was building up a tolerance for everything else . . . claimed he couldn't get kicks out of anything else. Holly, listen to me! Lee was high on speed — amphetamines — when he ran his bike over that cliff. I pleaded with him, lay off, slow down. He wouldn't listen. Seemed he wanted to cram every experience there was into a few short years. He wasn't ever going to be satisfied with his music. Nothing was ever going to satisfy him, and he knew it." Bart reached over to press Holly's wrist between his fingers. "I think he wanted to burn himself out. How were you and that old doctor supposed to know that accident was just a delay in a . . . in a deliberate collision course?"

"We should have known. We prided ourselves on knowing the whole patient," Holly remembered.

"Take this for what it's worth," Bart said. He released her wrist and sprang to his feet. "You *couldn't* 'ave known the whole of Lee Watson. Nobody ever did. Not even Lee."

He was moving away from her, and

Holly said, "Where are you going, Bart?"

"I just saw somebody I know." Bart turned back, twisting his homely face into a fond half-smile. "After I show him where you are, I can disappear into the woodwork or occupy myself doin' something useful. What say you give me your baggage checks and I rescue your luggage? Wouldn't do t' 'ave your toothbrush an' all flying off to America with you 'ere."

"But I'm not staying." Holly's protest sounded ludicrous, even to her own ears. "I have my ticket. I'm going —"

"I might as well get your ticket turned in, while I'm at it," Bart said. He held out his hand. Slowly, but not really hesitantly, Holly fished the ticket envelope and baggage receipt out of her handbag.

"You 'aven't really seen London, y'know," Bart said. "Pity to miss a bit of sightseeing. While you're here." He raced off before Holly could thank him, and before she could wax sentimental.

She watched Lee's quaintly dressed little manager dash toward the airline ticket window, only pausing to wave at someone else who was approaching. For, by that time, Glenn Raymond had spotted her, and he was hurrying, too.

Holly was walking toward him before

Glenn reached the waiting lounge. ...looked, strangely for a man who exemp...fied British reserve, as though he wer...racing to avert a catastrophe.

"Thank heaven you're still here!" Glenn exclaimed as he closed the distance between them. "Holly, you can't run off without listening to me. I don't deserve to be forgiven, but I can't let you go. Bart Mitchell can tell you —"

"He's already told me, Glenn."

"Told me, too. Though he didn't have to elaborate on what an idiot I am." Glenn ventured a hopeful smile. "That hurt, being true."

They were standing inches apart, their eyes locked, the magnetism between them making talk superfluous. "I don't have to tell you, do I? That I . . . didn't want to leave?"

"Do I have to tell you," Glenn asked in a gentle tone, "that I'm never going to let you go?"

She was in his arms, swept there with hardly a perceptible move between them. Glenn kissed her, and she let him hold her close, breathing a silent prayer of thanks for well-trained chauffeurs and managers who knew how to manage.

There were a million unresolved probs, she thought. It was a bit staggering think of spending the rest of your life in foreign land, even when it was a country you loved. Yet wouldn't she be willing to live anywhere, for the remainder of her days, if she could be at Glenn's side? There were unpleasant factors attached to her incredible inheritance, too. Bart would help her with advice. She could count on him now to solve any problems.

Perhaps Glenn was also thinking about the decisions they faced. On the other hand, perhaps he was too happy with the moment to concern himself with the future. He raised his lips from Holly's and pressed her closer. "Next to having you all to myself, I can't think of a better place than this, can you?"

Holly kissed him this time. No one was watching; intimate reunions and farewells were a matter of course at an airport terminal. "It's still legitimate," she said. "Until Bart gets back with my ticket refund. After that, we'll have to leave."

"It's too late in the day to stop for a wedding license," Glenn said. "Although I'm not so sure our little friend couldn't overcome that problem, too."

"Bart's done enough for us today," Holly said. "Can we wait until morning?"

"Just barely," Glenn warned her. Then, because there was no sign of Bart Mitchell, and, technically, Holly was still a departing passenger, Glenn kissed her once more. In a few minutes, she would be "coming back to London," he said, and he could greet her with his love. Tomorrow they would need no more excuses.